The Phototropic Woman

The Iowa School of Letters Award for Short Fiction

Prize money for the award is provided by a grant from the Iowa Art Council.

The Phototropic Woman

ANNABEL THOMAS

University of Iowa Press Iowa City

The previously published stories in this collection appear by permission:

"Ashur and Evir," *Bastian Review* (Fall 1972).

"The Hollyhock Doll," *Four Quarters* 22 (Summer 1973).

"The Great Tomato War," *Green River Review* 5 (Fall 1973).

"On Gobbler's Knob," *Four Quarters* 24 (Autumn 1974).

"Twister," *Forum* 15 (Winter 1974).

"Loaves and Fishes," *South Dakota Review* 13 (Summer 1975).

"The Other One," *Kansas Quarterly* 8 (Summer-Fall 1976).

"The Pinning," *Twigs* 13 (Fall 1976).

"Luther," *Epoch* (Winter 1976).

"Nativity," *Four Quarters* 26 (Summer 1977).

"Jerusha's Horses," *Green River Review* 10 (1979).

"Coon Hunt," *Epoch* (Spring 1978); *The O. Henry Prize Stories 1979* (New York: Doubleday).

"Margaret and Erdine," *Literary Review* 23 (Fall 1979).

"The Imprisoned Woman," *Prairie Schooner* 53 (Fall 1979).

"The Wellspring," *Forum* 20 (Winter 1979).

"The Phototropic Woman," *Wind/Literary Journal* 10 (1980); *The O. Henry Prize Stories 1981* (New York: Doubleday).

University of Iowa Press, Iowa City 52242

Printed in the United States of America

Library of Congress Cataloging in Publication Data

Thomas, Annabel, 1929-
The phototropic woman.

(The Iowa School of Letters award for short fiction)

I. Title. II. Series: Iowa School of Letters award for short fiction.

PS3570.H557P5 813'.54 81-10469

ISBN 0-87745-113-3 AACR2

ISBN 0-8745-114-1 (pbk.)

For Bill
who also unremittingly
seeks the light

Contents

1 / The Phototropic Woman
9 / Jerusha's Horses
15 / Twister
24 / The Other One
32 / Loaves and Fishes
42 / The Hollyhock Doll
54 / The Pinning
65 / Ashur and Evir
76 / The Great Tomato War
81 / Coon Hunt
89 / Margaret and Erdine
103 / Nativity
113 / On Gobbler's Knob
126 / Luther
142 / The Wellspring
160 / The Imprisoned Woman

The Phototropic Woman

The woman was rolled up in a woolen blanket. It covered her body and even her head so that her world was warm and soft as an unborn's. When the alarm went off, she got out of bed and poked up the stove.

She put water to heat and when it was steaming she stripped to the waist and washed in the basin. She pulled a sweater over her head and plaited up her hair. While she drank a mug of strong black tea, she read the survival book.

After she put the shack in order, the woman took a coil of rope and a box of candles and walked up the sun-speckled path through the locust thicket between the green mossed rocks big as sheep sheds. She had worn the path carrying and dragging the provisions the book recommended to the cave.

The cave smelt of damp sandstone and of dust and still air. She dropped the rope beside the boxes of canned goods and was counting the candles when she heard a noise like hundreds of nine pins falling onto a wooden floor. When she turned round she saw dirt and rock pouring into the mouth of the cave. Before she could move toward it, the opening was completely closed and she stood coughing in blackness.

The woman felt her way to the boxes and found the coal oil lantern and the matches. When the wick caught, the light reflected from a hundred rock surfaces overhead and around the edges while the middle was murky with floating dust. It was like standing inside a gem.

She took a pickax and dug where the entrance had been. She kept digging until she was too tired to dig any more.

"There's no use to that," the woman said.

In fact she wondered if she should try to get out at all, at least right away. Had she seen a flash of light just before the dirt came down? The woman stood still a long time thinking what she should do.

She began by pacing off the room. It was twenty by fifteen feet. Then she felt the roof, tracing it back to where it closed down like a clamshell.

She took the pickax and pried gently where the roof joined the floor. As she widened a crack in the stone she felt air rush through. She worked slowly and hesitantly, half afraid of digging out into poisoned air.

When the hole was large enough, she took the lantern and crawled into the opening. Working forward on her belly, she wriggled down through mud thick as grease. Her hair became caked and her clothes clogged with it. It went up her sleeves and down into her shoes.

The tunnel began to spiral like a corkscrew and to taper so that she got stuck sometimes, then squirmed loose and so at last came out of the tunnel onto the floor of a large room.

Wherever she shined the light she saw pillars with rock hanging from them in folds like cloth. She couldn't see the top of the room. She circled the walls. There was no way out except the way she'd come in.

Back in the upper room, she scooped out a trench with the pickax, laid large flat stones over the trench and closed the cracks with pebbles and mud. At the higher end she built a chimney from a small hollow tree limb. At the lower end she placed a handful of shredded bark and struck a match to it. She added twigs, then larger sticks from the supply of squaw wood she had gathered and stored in the cave. She kept the fire small. Every move she made came straight out of the survival book. She called up the pages in her mind's eye, then did what they said. When the fire burned steadily, she cooked soup.

Working and resting, then working again, the woman slowly enlarged the tunnel, hacking out hand holds and foot holds until she could pass up and down easily. At the far end of the lower room she found a trickle of water spreading thin and soundless over the face of the rock. She set a bucket to catch it where it dripped off a projection. By feeling her pulse, she calculated the minutes it took for the dripping water to fill the bucket. Each time she judged twenty-four hours had gone by she made a mark on the cave wall with a piece of sandstone. One day she totaled up the marks. She had been in the cave somewhat over twelve days.

As time passed, the woman gradually made herself a proper home in the upper room. She arranged the boxes for chairs and a table, cooked good meals on the fireplace she had built and after she had eaten, spread a blanket over the warm stones and slept.

She wondered what was going on outside. Was the world burnt to ashes? Were scarred people picking about through swelling corpses, twisted metal, broken glass? Or was everything as it had been and the sun shining calm and warm down through the leaves spotting the path. The thought of the sun gave her heart a twist as if a coal of fire had touched her in the breast.

Below the water trickle in the lower room, the woman discovered a small underground pool in a rock basin.

"The old fishing hole," she said for in the pool were strange white fish.

Instead of swimming away from her, they froze in the water when she reached for them. She seined them out easily with her skirt. They were three or four inches long. On either side of their heads, she found bulges covered with skin where the eyes had been.

She slit the fish open, gutted them and pinned them with thorns to a smooth log which she propped close to the fire. The book had told how.

"Survival," the woman said to the fish. "Mine, not yours."

On one of her fishing trips, she noticed, in a small recess filled with boulders on the far side of the pool, what appeared to be a piece of cloth caught beneath the bottom stone. It was of a coarse weave like burlap. She couldn't pull it free. Every day she passed by it she felt of the cloth.

"What is it?" she said.

Finally she took along the pickax and pried the boulders loose, rolling them off, one by one, across the floor. She worked gingerly, afraid of starting a cave-in and burying herself. As each boulder fell away, more of the cloth showed until she could see a large bundle wedged into a depression. She bent forward and lifted away the final stone, then started back, giving a little shriek.

"God in heaven," she said. "It's an Indian!"

"He won't scalp you," she added a moment later, peering down "He's been dead so long the meat's gone dry on his bones."

Although the long hair was much as it had been in life, the skin was blackish and hard and part of the skull was bare. The fiber blanket lay in patches over the rib cage. Beside the corpse was a small piece of gourd and a bundle of reeds tied together with grass.

"Came in out of a storm," the woman said, "and here he is still, poor bastard."

Leaning down to touch the Indian's blanket, the woman saw that the recess was a crawl way into yet another room.

She called the upper cave, "Home," and the second chamber, "the Indian Room." The third, the new one, became, "the Bat Room." The third room was fair sized though not so big nor so beautiful as the Indian Room. When the woman first heard the bats squeaking from a great distance overhead, she set the lantern on a rock and dug out handholds and footholds in the wall with a can lid. Following the method described in the survival book, she slapped the hand grips first and listened to hear if they sounded loose or cracked before going up carefully. She eased her foot into the vertical slits, twisting her ankle sideways, slipping in her toe, then straightening the ankle.

Now and then she paused in her climb to light a candle and have a look around. Once she saw a cave cricket, palest white and long-legged, creeping up the rock. Later she came upon the disintegrating body of a millipede with a white fungus encasing it like a shroud.

Pulling herself onto a ledge, she suddenly clapped her hands over her ears to shut out what sounded like the roaring of the biggest airplane motor in the world. Stretching her candle up at arm's length, she saw the bats, very high up, in a vast smoky cloud.

The ledge where she stood held a pool of bat droppings, a wide brown lake smelling of ammonia. As the candle light slid across it she saw it move. She bent over, shining the light full on it. It was seething with living creatures. Tens of thousands of beetles, flat worms, snails, millipedes, and mites were swimming on the surface or crawling on the bottom of the guano. All of them were colorless and all of them were blind.

Where the bats came in, she couldn't tell. She felt no air and saw no light. When the rock of the walls grew too hard to dig, she had to climb back down. She never came in sight of the ceiling.

Next she explored a number of small passageways opening off the Bat Room. Most dead-ended, choked with fallen rock. The rest opened onto horrifying drops. One descended and became an underground stream which she waded until the roof closed down to the water. Then she turned back.

The woman now believed that she had examined every room and passageway accessible to her and that there was no way out of the cave.

She settled into a routine of fishing, cooking, eating, and sleeping. Time flowed on, sluggish and slow. She hung in it, drowsily.

But she dreamed strange dreams. And all her dreams were about light. At first she couldn't remember them but woke with only the imprint of brightness on her eyes like an aftertaste on the tongue.

Later, she recalled scenes in which she lay doubled inside a giant egg, walled away from the light. As she beat on the shell, stretching toward the light, she could feel the light outside straining toward her. At last, with a cracking like a mighty explosion, she straightened her arms and legs sending the shell into bits. As she thrust forth into hot brightness, she looked to see if it were the sun or the flash of an explosion that beat upon her but she never found out.

When the coal oil was gone and the woman began to use the candles more and more sparingly, the shape of day and night blurred and faded from her life. Her meals became irregular. She ate as often as she felt hungry. Sometimes she forgot to eat at all for long stretches. She let the bucket overflow or forgot to mark on the wall so often that at last she lost all track of how long she had been in the cave.

Once, as she opened a can by candlelight, she lifted the lid and looked at her reflection in the shiny tin circle.

She saw that her face and arms had grown pasty. Her clothes were colorless from dirt and wear. She had broken her glasses when she climbed the wall of the Bat Room so that she peered at herself through eyes slightly out of focus. The skin hung loose on her cheeks and drew taut across the sharp bridge of her nose. Her hair, trailing loose on her shoulders, was pale with dust.

The candle sputtered, brightened, then, burned to its end, died. She reached for another. The candles rattled against one another in the box. So few left? Her hands shook, counting them. How many more hours of light? Not many. Then the dark.

As the woman let the candles fall from her fingers, a strange restlessness came upon her. She moved to the cave mouth and felt of the mass of dirt and rock which covered it. She caught up the pickax and dug until she couldn't lift it for another stroke.

After that she often counted the candles and as often dug at the entrance. Blisters broke on her hands and bled. Sweat dripped off her chin. Her body burned. It was as if she felt the light through the tons of dirt over her head, pulling her toward it whether she wanted to go or not. She dug until her arm went numb. Then she threw herself on the floor and slept. When she woke, she dug again.

Sometimes she dropped the pickax and fell to tearing at the dirt and rocks with her fingers. Afterwards she cleaned her hands and wrapped them in strips she tore from her skirt.

At last she left off digging and circled the Indian Room and the Bat Room each in turn again and again, feeling of the walls, climbing where she could gouge out a hand and foothold, going as far up as she was able, then dropping back.

Next she re-examined each of the passageways at the end of the Bat Room. One passage ended in a shallow pit carved into the stone with walls round like a chimney and stretching up out of sight. Down this chimney, it seemed to the woman, there poured like steady rain a strange dark light.

She placed her back against one wall of the chimney and lifted both her feet onto the wall opposite. She pressed a hand against the rock on either side of her buttocks and so levered her body off the wall. She inched her way up, alternately pressing her feet against one wall and her back against the other. Soon the chimney narrowed so that she was forced to use her knees instead of her feet and after a time she began to slip.

She slid down, caught herself, and started up once more. Her back and knees were raw and bleeding. The portions of her sweater and skirt covering them had worn away. She slipped again, reached out her hands to catch herself, tried to hold onto the sides of the pit, could not, and fell heavily, shot down like a stone, and hit the cave floor with a yell loud enough to wake the dead Indian.

When she tried to stand, the woman's ankle wouldn't bear her weight. It took her a long time to drag herself back to the Home Chamber. Once there, she mixed a poultice of mud and spread it on the ankle from the middle of the calf to the instep. Gradually it hardened into a cast.

The woman lay wrapped in her blanket on the warm stones while, slowly, her bruises and scrapes began to heal. She had used to talk to herself aloud a good part of the time. Now, she fell deeper and deeper into silence until her thoughts lost the shape of words and shot through her brain in strange flashes of feeling and impulse.

In her dreams she repeated the accident and repeated it, always waking with the sensation of having been, in falling, drenched with light. She slept, woke, ate, slept again. Her ankle ached less, then not at all. When she judged enough time had passed, the woman took a small stone and pounded the mud cast gently so that it cracked and fell away. She walked up and down the home cave until her ankle grew strong.

When she was able to return to the Indian Room and the Bat Room, she again explored the walls and passages, ending at last with the underground river. She waded the stream to the point where the overhead rocks narrowed down to touch the water. The river deepened as the roof came down so that she stood in water to her armpits.

She filled her lungs and swam downstream under the rocks. Feeling with her fingers that the roof still touched the water and still touched and still touched, she swam back.

She tried again. Then again. Before each try she breathed in and out rapidly and so was able to stay under water longer. With each attempt she went further until, when she felt the roof begin to rise, she pushed on and broke from the water into a narrow tunnel with air at the top and headroom enough to stand upright.

Back in the Home Chamber, the woman took the rope into her lap. She ran a few feet of its cold damp length through her fingers. The day she had carried it to the cave, it had been warm from the sun. She tore a strip from the bottom of her blanket and tied it to the rope. She added another strip and another until she had tied on the whole of the blanket.

At the river, she knotted one end of the rope around her waist and looped the other over a rock projection. Wading slowly downstream, she felt a slight push of current at the backs of her legs. Her thigh touched a fish hanging still in the water.

Swimming to the spot where she had stood before, she walked on in waist-high water. She could reach out her hands and touch both walls of the tunnel that held the river. The roof hung a few feet above her.

The woman moved on in blackness, trailing the rope. When she rubbed her eyes she saw pale flashes far back inside her head.

Several yards beyond the point where she'd turned back before, she began to feel the roof closing rapidly down again, grazing her head so that she must stoop to go forward. When her feet lost touch with the bottom she began to swim.

The water was numbing cold. Her clothes hung on her like the metal plates of a suit of armor. Only her head was above water and still the roof brushed her hair and she felt it closing, closing.

The woman took several quick, deep breaths, filled her lungs, and dove down through the water. Leveling off, she shot ahead rapidly, keeping a steady forward push with arms and legs, hands and feet. She continued on for the length of her body, then her body's length again. And again. As she swam she waited for the tug at her waist that would tell her she had reached the rope's end, the point of no return. When it came, she slipped the knot and swam out of the rope, leaving it to curl in the water behind her.

Her lungs began to ache in earnest. The blood, pounding behind her eyes, filled her head with glances of bright color. Stubbornly she kept up her steady breast stroke, her frog kick, until the expanding and contracting of her muscles became the structure of her consciousness.

She tried to remember her life outside the cave but she could not. She tried to recall the details of her days in the Home Chamber, the Indian and the Bat Rooms but they were washed from her brain leaving only the sensation of inward scalding light creating, destroying her in its struggle to be born.

Jerusha's Horses

Jerusha woke to a galloping, light and swift as rain, and to a far off whickering.

She crossed the floor on bare feet and, from the high window, watched for them to break, first one, then another, into the streets and onto the brick walks under the light pole.

Soon they would come. Now. Now. Shoulder to shoulder, black and white, bay and piebald, sweeping down the street, the Appaloosas, the tear-drop horses, in the lead, neighing with wide nostrils. Soon she would jump onto their backs and ride to a far country.

When they came at last, windows would go up, sashes slamming. People would stick out their heads, crying to one another, "The horses! The horses!" and from the doors the scoffers would run, pouring onto the lawns, stumbling in their hurry, racing, sprinting after the horses. But Jerusha and the horses would flash away like fire in a wind leaving only the hoof-raised dust settling on their faces as they moved about left behind amongst the steaming droppings.

However, this time the sound of horses was gone as quickly as it had come. Not a whisper left in all the silent street. No one looked out. No one heard. Only herself whose blood still knocked with the rhythm of the horses.

Jerusha put back the wire mesh where she had loosened it secretly from the window and got into her gown, buttoning it up rich man poor man all the way to Indian chief. It was Grampop, the son of a chief, who used to tell Jerusha about the horses, how their manes snapped in the wind, how their tails stood like flags, how they blackened the plains with their great numbers.

Blue afternoon light washed the room. Outside, no horses were in sight. Jerusha tiptoed to the door. The gum wrappers she'd packed into the latch had kept the lock from snapping shut. The door swung in when she pulled it. A little more. A little more but slowly because the hinges squealed. When there was room enough, she wiggled out. Down the hall patting light on carpet. The stone steps were cold. Going down, she curled her toes over the edges, feeling the dip in the stone made by all the feet through all the years.

She went first to the day room where the children were and sat down on the floor, unnoticed because she was nearly as small as they and the bottoms of her feet were dirty like theirs and they all wore the same green wrappers.

First one then another of the little ones came crawling into her lap and when it was full, others leaned over her shoulders or rolled at her feet and she began to tell them about the horses. The children that banged their heads or tore their hair stopped and the ones that shouted were still and the ones that never talked held their breath, listening.

She told about the horses' nostrils, how they were soft as a lady's cheek, how they moved in and out like wings beating, how long hairs grew on their chins and how their great eyes were bluish in the center like pools where hidden fish were swimming.

Some children remembered favorites and asked her to talk about them: a black with a white star on his forehead and three white stockings, an albino with wild pink eyes, a roan sprinkled with white hairs like salt.

She said to them that when Grampop sent the horses to fetch her, she'd give each child a horse to keep and still there would be horses left over.

The children's bodies were warm on hers as if she stood already in the midst of the horses, and she sang them a song about the horses that Grampop had sung to her when they lived together in the shack by the river.

Hark! Tat-tat-a-tat. Hooves in the streets. The children, listening, thought they heard, too. They all went to the mesh-covered window but to the east and to the west were only empty brick walks, empty lawns, empty asphalt streets.

At the window, the children pressed against Jerusha so her breath squeezed out in gasps. There was such a commotion, such arguments who should have her right hand and who her left that they came and took the children away, feeding them pills and soothing syrups and giving them shots for sleep.

They found Jerusha wrapped in children. They gripped her arms with rough fingers but she twisted free and ran off through the door and away fast as the Appaloosas around the windings of the corridors until they were left behind, puffing. Only their sounds trailed after her, the clucking of tongues like those who came to the shack and said, "Pigsty," because Grampop spat tobacco juice, "Starving," because he and Jerusha ate dandelions greens. "Senile." "Idiot." "To the boneyard." "To the boobyhatch." Months and years Grampop kept them off but at last neither shouting nor stomping stopped it from happening.

In front of Jerusha now was the folding iron gate. Hard to get through but it could be done by sitting in shadow, walking on air, waiting the right tick, the right tock.

First time, second time, third time the screaming nakeds had scratched her, beat her bruised and smarting, ripped her gown, pulled out her hair in handfuls. The quiets, chins down on their collarbones, looking inside their heads, didn't notice.

But now they all knew her. Dimly, as plants know the sun, they stretched toward her coming, turned with her passing, bowed after her going.

Once inside she leaned against the wall telling them in a whisper about the horses. The screamers fell silent, squatting on their haunches and the still ones moved their gaze up along the inside of their skulls, out of the eye sockets, toward her mouth.

She told about the great pounding hearts of the horses squeezing tight, dropping loose under their ribs as they moved, of their broad chests many times wider than both her hands opened out thumb to thumb, and the wonderful heat of their bodies that rose from their flanks so that the air around them shimmered like water.

She told how they were coming to her straight from Grampop like breath from his nostrils, like glances from his eyes, like hot blood from his veins, to sweep her off to the high plains where he was already waiting for her, standing by the burial scaffold.

Listening, the sound of sighing moved through the room like a rising wind so that all shook and fluttered as birds longing for flight and reached out to pluck her. She gave each of them a horse though the herd, certainly coming, was a long way off, but impatient, they began to howl and bang against the iron gate until, snaking down the hall, the hose came squirting water hard as stones.

When the gate was opened, Jerusha rolled out through ankles and down, bumping, step to step, into the basement, undetected.

Clashing forks, rattling cups, the scoffers ate and drank, dressed in caps and aprons or high collars, white pants or white hose.

Near the coffee urn she looked ordinary and began to hand out rolls with a pair of silver tongs putting them on round blue saucers and placing them in the reaching fingers, listening as they dropped in money, jingling.

The smoke from fifty cigarettes rose like chaff and the puffers dropped down, each one winnowed, hard-coated, on the stony floor and, unbelieving, never sprouted.

Better be still, beware, be wary. And would have, had she not, pitying them, left the rolls and sat down at a table amongst them and begun to talk about the horses.

"What horses?" they asked, blank-faced. "No horses around here except at the track. You play the daily double?"

"No horses. Plenty of horse shit, though."

"And horse play."

"And horsing around."

"And Charley-horses."

Before she could stop herself she mentioned the skin soft as mullen leaves that moved of itself, the pricking, pointed ears, the everlasting thighs and the rumble of their gallop like a thousand voices speaking the same word over and over in unison.

At once they said, "By god, we know you! You're Crazy Jerusha from Five-A loose again!" and grabbed but she moved quick out of their reach and stood in the door, listening. Some were afraid and ran out the back crying save us and some laughed, rolling on the floor and the rest came after her, saying—

"Enough is enough."

Jerusha ran up the stairs, climbing. They, puffing and wheezing, came close behind, reaching.

And even then would have given them a horse each, saving them, but they . . . .

Down the corridors, her legs pumping, upsetting mop buckets, food trays, wheelchairs. Through the walls she heard the horses, closer now, like drums beating and stopped and tried to open paint-frosted panes but here the metal mesh wouldn't budge. She tugged until her fingers bled, ran on knowing now where to go, up more stairs and in where they wanted her but they weren't satisfied, trying to follow her. She pushed the dresser against the door and the bed against the dresser wedged tight so they stopped, milling about in the hall.

While they pounded at the door, the night rolled in with a scent of sweating horses. She looked out the window, staring down. Empty brick walks. Silent streets. Still trees. But no horses. Where?

Pulled up the loosened mesh, crawled out on the ledge, rose, swaying, to her feet on the narrow stone strip, gazing up, head bent back, eyes traveling like a child's eyes up a body's length to find a face. Up. High. Higher.

And saw the stars. Saw a thousand. Saw a million million. Pricks of light. Points of flame. Darts. Sparks. Flares. Glances. Eyes. Horses' eyes shining as they galloped helter-skelter down the sky.

Buckskin, black, brown, white palamino, bay, dark bay, blood bay, liver chestnut, golden chestnut, sorrel, dun, dapple grey, skewbald, piebald, pied, roan: racking now, tails up, manes flying.

She braced herself against the wall and leaned out, breathless, to watch them sweep nearer. Now their hooves touched the streets, now the brick walks, striking sparks. Past the corner. Past the light pole. Along the hedge.

"The horses! The horses!"

Her voice spurred those in the hall to great effort. A splintering of wood. The bed, the dresser knocked aside, the door flung open, steps across the floor.

Fingers plucked at her shoulders, closed on her gown. She shrugged out of it, left it behind like a shed skin when she dropped from the ledge just as, clipping-clopping with a sound like dice rattling, bones shaking, scissors sharpening, water flowing, the horses swept beneath.

Down past the fourth floor windows, third, second, first. Already with them, she felt the heat rising from their backs, smelled the grass-sweet breath from their nostrils, touched at last the soft dusty hides with her outstretched toes, her fingertips, her hands, arms, with her bare knees, her thighs, and, settling astraddle, moved with them off through the tender night.

Twister

The piquant child leaned out the door calling, "Come, Gibbet, come!"

The woman, tall and broad of shoulder, turned from her loom to watch the child, a shadow settling in her clear eyes. "The cat won't come, Margaret," she said.

"Why not?"

"She's gone away."

"Where?"

"Away. Step outdoors and tell me: is it going to rain? What do you think?" The woman waited good-humoredly while her child ran out into the yard and stared up at the sky.

"It's not raining now."

"But will it, do you think?"

"No. It won't."

"Because you want it shouldn't?"

"No. Because I'm sure it won't. There's only a little cloud on the sun."

"Then we'll go."

Jane Geist passed the shuttle once more between the warp threads and laid it on top of the loom. Beneath, the yarns were twisted into a simple patterned fabric. The warp was white and the weft black. The woman had learnt the craft of her granny. She made a few blankets and rugs now and again for what money they brought and for the pleasure of the work. She stood up, stretching her strong arms.

"Fetch my jacket, Ma."

"Yes. And then we'll start."

Jane pulled on her own wrap, handed the child her jacket, and stood waiting. The little girl held out her jacket and thrust her arm through the sleeve. "No, that's wrong. You'll have it backwards."

Again the child put in her arm.

"No. Take the short side, Margaret."

Tears of vexation started in the little girl's eyes. "You help, Ma."

Jane took the jacket and with a respectful air held it while her daughter stuck in one arm and then the other. "Now we're ready," she said taking up her husband's lunch pail from the table.

The two passed out of the house and over the yard by the barn and so into the woods. For several yards through the woods Margaret went along looking under the bushes and behind the trees calling, "Come, Gibbet. Come, Gibbet." At last, growing tired of the bootless search she squatted down by a sumac bush watching a spider strap the leaves one to another in an intricate design.

"Now that's a present for you," Jane said seriously as the wind fluttered the web. "A glad sight on a dark day."

"See," said Margaret.

"Yes. But I can't get so close," Jane laughed, continuing on her way. "I can't squinch down like you."

"Why not?"

"Because you are four and I'm forty-five and my back hurts me. You're the child of my old age, Margaret. You've got to be patient."

The child ran here and there among the trees. Now and again the sun, as it dipped in and out of the clouds, caught in the fine yellow mist of her hair.

What a tiny mite she was and how intense! Her mother followed after her, amused, marveling. After so many years to have such a child! Jane's being thawed and lightened at the sight of her. Surely marking Margaret running ahead she beheld a bright living piece of her own soul moving free. She continued on dreamily. "Look here," she said suddenly, bending down and plucking a leaf. "Put this in your mouth and chew it."

"It's tea," said the child, tasting.

"Well then, you're a smart cookie because you're right. It's sassafras. I used to chew it in the woods when I was little. On the way back we'll dig some roots."

"Do this, Ma," Margaret cried suddenly grabbing her mother's hand and laying one large blunt finger on her own forehead.

"But we must hurry to Pa."

"No. Do this."

"Pa's been plowing since daybreak. You and me's got to fetch him his pail. He's hungry."

"Do this."

"All right," Jane looked into her daughter's solemn bright little face and began pointing out her features slowly one by one. "Forehead backer, eye winker, tom tinker, nose dropper, mouth eater, chin chopper." Here Margaret began to squeal and scream and to tuck down her chin against the tickling "Gulley, gulley, gulley!" which came anyway.

"Do it again."

Jane kissed her daughter solemnly on the vein in the warm inside bend of her arm.

"No. Run on."

"I spoil her," the mother thought wistfully. "I keep her by me and pet her and talk to her minute by minute. But she lifts me so." "Listen to this," she called suddenly to Margaret and she raised her hands and cupping them blew upon her thumbs sending forth a low penetrating whistle. "Now, hark."

Mother and daughter stood quite motionless, listening. Soon an answering whistle came from far away through the trees.

"That was your Pa," Jane said, nodding. "Now he knows we're coming."

"I want to blow."

"You're too small to make a peep. Well then, you see, you must hold your hands so. No, palm to palm. Bend your thumbs."

Margaret grew very red in the face from blowing through her hands. "I can't."

"Keep trying. It'll come."

"No. I can't." The child stamped her foot and blew and blew.

"Try this then," said the mother, amused and patient but pitying her. She reached out with her strong arms and lifted Margaret up to the top branches of a young sapling.

"Now catch hold the top there. Grip on tight."

Jane let the child go so that she swung out, her thin legs kicking free in the air. Slowly the limber trunk bowed lower and yet lower until its leafy top branches touched the ground, rustling. Margaret found her footing and let go the tree and it sprang back into the air, quivering. "Do it again."

"No. Now we've got to get on. My dad licked me for bending down the trees."

"Did you play with the trees, Ma, when you were little like me?"

"Yes. And I dammed up the creek and waded. I picked wild flowers and stood them in jars. I found fairy rings where the toad stools grow in a circle. I made cups and saucers out of acorns. We'll fetch some home and I'll show you. The woods is full of play things. Or you can work and sing and dance all yourself and that's a plenty to fill your days with."

The trees began to thin out as they approached the field. Mother and daughter moved along content and watchful. The child went and stood by a tree, excitedly feeling at the bark, crying, "Make a whistle, Ma."

Jane laughed out, throwing back her broad shoulders. "You know what a willow is, but I ain't got a knife this trip. Look here where the trees is scarce. There's sweet william and here's spring beauties blooming and bloodroot. Look for a trillium but don't pull it off else it'll wither."

Margaret dropped to her knees and began to search among the leaves while her mother continued on to the field. Jane went with her heart yearning backward to the little one. What a spark of life she was with her quick thin little body and her cloud of fine hair. How nimbly she doubled up squatting among the fragile woods posies.

Suddenly the woman's being ached with an extremity of love as swollen in her as a milk-full breast yet unsucked. The child and the flowers roused her so. She looked back from the edge of the field and saw them perfectly, nestled in the dappling shadow under the branches. She stood comprehending them deeply, immersed in their eternal reality.

Her husband walked behind the horses, the leather lines tied behind his hips, guiding the plow with his familiar, weathered hands around the hill field which rose too steep for the use of a tractor.

"Bob," she called and he left the plow and came to her stepping wide across the turned earth, while behind him the horses rested in the traces with their heads down. She handed him the pail.

"Where's Margaret?"

"At the edge of the woods there."

"The wind's uncommon strong."

"Yes."

"Bet and Dolly is skittish. There's maybe a storm coming."

"I don't think so."

"Well."

"You're tired, old man," she said tenderly. His shirt was black with sweat over his bony shoulders and his mouth lay lax where the tobacco juice stained the corners.

"Yes, old woman," he said, smiling a little but straightening himself and strong enough still and content.

"Now then I'll take the horses around while you eat."

"There's no need."

"I like to do it. If you finish by sundown you can plant tomorrow as you've been fretting to do."

"Yes."

He sat on a stump and ate watching his wife follow the horses around the field. The wind pressed her dress to her long thighs. He saw her shoulders strong and heavy as she pulled back on the lines. Her eyes were on the point of the plow where it parted the furrow. She came round once and yet again.

"Jane."

"Yes."

"Now give the horses a drink and let them rest."

She unhitched them from the plow and led the great ponderous beasts to the spring down the field's edge. She let them blow, tethered there.

"Listen at this, Jane."

"Why, what's the matter?"

"Hark over yonder in the trees."

Man and wife stood still, listening. Margaret's voice came to them carried piping and frail on the wind.

"Here, Gibbet. Here, Gibbet."

"Well," said Jane, troubled but not owning it. "And so she calls the cat."

"You had ought to tell her it's dead, Jane."

"No."

"Yes. You know you had ought."

"She'd only grieve her soul over it."

"And so she should."

"Still, I pity her."

"You can't keep her from death, Jane."

"I can for a little."

"She should know young that the wild dogs will gut a kitten. It's a natural end."

"It's a shame, too."

Bob looked at his wife. Her large strong face was flushed with the plowing. Perspiration stood on her lip and he shook his head and laughed at her. "You're a lively woman, Jane," he said.

Weak and foolish with the pleasure of the food in his belly and the relief of resting his body after the long morning's labor, he delighted in her and how her concern was all with life. Her body exuded life. There was no room for death in her.

"I am, yes," she answered him calmly.

"You're alive every inch. You can outplow any man that lives."

"Yes."

"But you shelter Margaret too much. You do too much for her. You don't let her learn to do for herself, for you and for other folks as well. You must let her alone to sorrow or laugh as it comes to her. You protect her overly, I think, Jane. You teach her about life but you hide away death. She should know both as they're threads of the same cloth. She must learn to live with dying all around her, you know. That's how we all must learn to live."

"Why, yes," Jane said, weary of the bootless talk. "I'll tell her about the cat, then."

Satisfied, Bob went to hitch the horses once more to the plow. As Jane turned from him, she saw Margaret coming out of the woods, her short skirts held to her waist and filled with wild blossoms. The wind swept her along and lifted her hair like a bit of fluff. "See, Ma?" she piped gladly.

"I see. Come down to the spring, Margaret, and we'll soak the stems and wrap them in wet leaves so they won't fade," Jane said.

They went along the edge of the field together stepping where the live warm earth was turned up to the sun waiting to receive the seed. Then, the flowers cool and dripping, mother and daughter took their way slowly home through the darkening wind-whipped forest stopping to pull up sassafras roots along the path and to gather acorns among last fall's leaves. Dusk fell early that evening and the family ate supper with the lamps lit. Afterwards Bob smoked his pipe on the porch, watching the clouded western sky which remained red long after the sun had set.

Late that night Margaret awoke to find that the light in the hall was not burning. She sat up, wide awake, and called out but no one came. It was strangely close and hot. Sweat trickled down the child's neck from under the short fine cloud of her hair. "Ma."

No one answered.

And "Ma, Ma," the child called again kicking her thin short legs over the edge of the bed and sliding to the floor in the dark. Through the open window she could see the wind behaving like an angry puppy, tearing at the trees. She could hear it worrying the walls of the house until they groaned.

Margaret padded up to the window. Lightening flashed unnaturally in an intermittent brightness as if someone were switching a light quickly on and off and yet again on. She saw that the sky was glowing in colors behind the clouds. "Pa."

She went down the stairs and her parents were nowhere. The wind banged and shouted. "Ma, Pa," she said and opened the door and went out into the yard. Margaret was rather frail and small of frame. The wind nearly sucked her up. The limb of a tree twice the size of her leg tumbled past her left ear and went bouncing off across the barn lot.

Intent of purpose she continued on to the barn. Her face was expressionless and absorbed like a small fetus. She was outraged that her parents did not come. She was awestruck by her own fear at their absence which was very great. She found that she could not open the barn door. As she stood tugging at it, silent and numb, overwhelmed by the strangeness of being out-of-doors at night, a spider dropped suddenly from the door onto her arm, crept over her hand and away. Then, although it was May, hail began to rattle on the ground. It stung the child's bare ankles. Margaret saw it plainly in the lightning flashes which came always closer together. She watched, all at once delighted as the small white balls jumped about at her feet.

She started when the wind fairly shook the barn from side to side and up and down. There was the sound of a deep-throated roaring. She listened openmouthed. The wind roared exactly like a train. "Ma!" Margaret worked at the handle on the barn door and suddenly the entire door pulled from her and went sailing off loose and free, spinning around and around up over her head and away. The air was filled with flying boards and shingles from the walls and roof of the barn.

The heavy-handed wind passed away quickly and rain began to fall.

Margaret stood blinking, looking with a puzzled expression at the space where the barn had been. When the rain had wet her through, she was cold and she began to cry. It took her a long time to return to the house since a tree had been uprooted between house and barn and she must crawl through the dripping branches. It was a useless effort since the house too was gone. Only the cellar remained yawning darkly at her feet.

Two men from the nearby village found her there in the morning sitting quietly in her nightdress on the edge of the cellar with her small hands folded in her lap. They spoke to her gently. They wished to question her but she paid them no mind. They could not catch her eye. Instead she looked off toward the woods.

They turned away from her to stare about. Debris covered the grass: broken two-by-fours, shards of roofing, a splintered table. A frying pan was lodged in the crotch of a tree. A piece of the loom lay tangled in the uprooted tree's branches, a few threads of the warp yarn still hanging to the frame.

One man lowered himself into the cellar.

"They're down here," he said almost at once.

"Oh God. I can see them," the man above cried out. "I can see them from here."

"They're both down here and they're both dead," the man below went on wonderingly. "There's kerosene all over the floor under these boards and a busted lantern. They never knew what hit the place. They was trying to fill the lantern when the house blew in on top of them."

"Then why is the little girl alive? There ain't a mark on her."

"She wasn't in the house. She couldn't have been and lived. She must have been outside some way or other."

"Ain't that odd?"

"It is. But then the funnel was odd. It skipped over the village except for the west edge. It took off a few roofs on the west edge."

Before removing the bodies from the cellar, the two men picked up the small girl and carried her to their car where they doubled her up in a blanket and placed her on the seat. "Now who'll raise her?" one man asked. "She's got no kin I've heard about."

"God knows," said the other.

When they had finished and returned to the car, they found the child had not moved. She still crouched, blanket-wrapped as they had left her. Only the ends of her yellow hair lifted and fell on her shoulders stirred by a morning breeze.

The Other One

My death will come walking toward me like a black dog.

Wileem hung by her heels from the telephone wires imitating an aerialist. She wore only a faded Mother Hubbard and her breasts swung loose and free beneath the bodice.

My love is a boy on a bicycle who gave me a half-eaten stick of candy and pedaled on, thin-shouldered, down the road.

Wileem spun around on her toes on the ceiling bright and smooth with morning light. The window was open and she could hear river noises through the early still.

She slid out of bed and ran to the window. Far far down and below the house the river ran, muddy but pure. The little boats glided down it catching the sun on their decks. While Wileem watched, the fog stretched and rose from the river bed and stood upright, weaving in sleepy spirals.

In the middle of the river a raft slipped slowly by and a black man stood on it singing. From the river bank where women were washing clothes, a high voice cut into his on the wonderfully quiet air.

Lord God have mercy on us poor sinners but I wisht I was a black man floating down the river. I wisht I was a washer woman in love with the river. Oh you pretty O-hi-oh.

The deep song and the high song spread out over the river and licked back solemn and ponderous. They fought together, work song and river song, settled their differences, flowed together and became another thing.

Wileem, new as the morning, turned back into the room.

I've fell in the river and I've drowned, good Lord. I'll hunt my love floating on a catfish. I'll wash my clothes in the cold brown muddy. I'll sing glory floating down to Mobile. That black man kissed the river with his voice as deep as a drum and it licked his feet.

The other one sat up in bed and said nothing.

But when she ran downstairs and out into the wet grass to feel the dark dew on her feet, the sunlight was green with a storm coming on and unnatural. The river below broke white and made an ugly noise.

Something, something, something violent is going to—.

Her aunt grabbed her by the arm with a hot hand.

"Little bitch. What you a-doing?"

Aunt Lila, fat with penciled black eyebrows and sunken cheeks, square shoulders, and a voice as deep as a man's.

"I ain't a-doing nothing."

"What you got in yore hand? Here. Lemme see it. Give it hyar, I say."

Smack. Across the face with her hot hand.

"Gum. Chewing gum. Where'd you git it?"

"Lemme be, Aunt."

"I seen Jarvie Wills drive away from here last night. Don't think I didn't. He give it ter you."

"He th'owed it to me, driving past, was all."

"Likely. You whore-bitch. Nakit under that rag, I 'low. I know about you."

Wileem pulled away raking the skin off her arm on her aunt's clutching fingernails. The air's wetness sopped up her breath.

"He's a fine gentleman, Jarvie is."

"He's a bastard that's heered of you, is all."

"He's a hightone man that's crazy in love of me."

"He's heered about yore goings ons with the army camp down the river, is all."

"He's coming to call some evening. He bought a new pistol, all silver, he's going to show me and beg to be my love."

"Get in the house an' get yore sister up."

"You lemme be. If Ma and Pa had a-lived — ."

"I'd be happy, Lord, cause you'd be dirtying their house and their name, rest they souls, not mine."

Wileem went in and up the stairs.

No man ever looked at your fat is why. And I'm pretty, pretty, pretty is why. They all love me to pieces. Jarvie, don't beg me. I gotta think over being your wife. I got to think if my love is deep enough. Deep as where the channel cats swim. There was a albino catfish once Jake Watt caught. All the people admired it so.

Up in the tiny bedroom smelling of unwashed clothes and Wileem's musk-heavy perfume, the other one lay looking at the green light on the ceiling as the storm gathered.

Wileem dressed herself and poured perfume in her hair. She threw the covers up over her bed. Then she turned to the other one, shaking her.

"Get up, Sister. Get up."

The other one got out of bed slowly. Her face was strange in the green light: sharp and small and without expression except for quick little animal eyes that followed after Wileem. She was a woman perhaps ten years older than Wileem.

"Get up, Sister. Did you know we got mush for breakfast? And today something, something, something's going to happen? Jarvie will buy me a ice cream maybe.

"Did you know it's going to storm? They holy Jesus gonna drownd the earth maybe. We'll sleep in the cold water. Did you know you're a bed post? You're a tree stump.

"Did you know Aunt hates us and all them river people hates us and the Jesus gospel singers hates us and the soldier boys hates us with crooked eyes. But I'm pretty, pretty, pretty and you're a bed post. Come on, Sister."

The other one followed Wileem downstairs.

After breakfast, Wileem and her sister ran bare-legged down the hill to the store. The strange too bright sun gathered itself up in the other one's face and shone over her cheek bones.

"Hello, pretty boy. Hello, pretty boy," Wileem called to the farmers driving up to the store in team-drawn wagons.

They said, "Hello, Wileem."

"Hello, Bluebell," said Wileem to the girl clerk whose name was Jane and who was thin and had buck teeth. "Aunt wants a side of salt pork and a sack of corn meal."

The sister stood beside Wileem with no expression on her face.

"Was your aunt mad when you got home so late from the dance last Saturday?" the girl said, measuring the yellow corn meal.

"Lord no, Bluebell. She was sick worried for fear I had broke my leg or some such but so glad to see me she just come apart. She loves me to pieces."

"I've heered different, Wileem."

"She just wants me to sit by of her side and read to her the day long, she's so crazy to have me close."

"You never finished enough school to read much, Wileem. You should ought to be going now."

"I kain't because Aunt wants me with her. Sister wants a candy stick."

My love was a boy on a bicycle who gave me—.

As they climbed back up the hill, a jeep-load of soldiers passed them on the way to town yelling,

"Hey, Wileem."

But the tone of their voices made her lower her head and keep her eyes on the ground. The other one, whose light red hair fuzzed out from her thin milk white face, swiveled her neck, staring first after the soldiers and then at Wileem.

Then Jarvie Wills, who had been drinking whiskey, came barreling up the road and stopped with a clatter and a clang. Wileem climbed on the door and the other one stood watching with quick eyes but didn't say anything.

"Jarvie, honey, I do believe it's going to storm."

The green sky made him look wicked like a bank robber in a movie. He reached out and put his hand on Wileem's knee and she let him.

"When's that damned battleax going away?"

"You mean Aunt? She don't like to leave me alone."

"Your foot. She noises all over creation how she got stuck with you two. She says right out she hates your guts."

"Where's your new pistol?"

"Never mind."

"Will you let me shoot it off?"

"We'll see."

"Is it pretty silver?"

"Yes. Why don't she ever say nothing? Her, there?"

Wileem turned and stared at the other one. A cold wind had sprung up and was blowing her tangled red hair wild. Her face was without expression or age or meaning.

"She kain't."

"What do you mean, she can't?"

"She ain't like a real person. She ain't never said nothing. She's a deaf-dummy."

"Oh."

"I got to git on."

"When can I come?"

"Tonight. Come tonight. When the moon comes up. Aunt goes to Jesus Revival then."

The long afternoon flowed over Wileem deep and muddy like the river. She lay barelegged and drowsy under the pear tree and saw its silver leaves flicking. The other one watched Wileem out of her quick animal eyes. Wileem dozed and prattled in her sleep.

There's the pretty mother and she looks like someone I know and her grave mound's wet with crying for me. This time it'll be different, I know, Lord Jesus. It'll be lovely. He loves me to pieces. Do quit begging me, Jarvie. I got to consider. That angel mother is hovering in the pear tree. I hear her wings. Oh, I hear her silver wings.

And Wileem awoke all in a sweat, wide-eyed, weak and shaking and felt as if she'd had a vision and spoken in tongues and she trembled and was afraid.

Aunt put on her blue handkerchief over her hair and took her Bible and hymnbook and went down the hill. After a while through the dusk, voices floated up shouting and sobbing and laughing together in gospel song. The cold wind rattled the trees and swept the river that was black now and bobbing with lights.

Wileem stared at the sky and it was flecked with grey-green

cloud bits and the only way she knew the moon was behind them was by a growing lumination that lit the black hills and crept inside her soul.

Glory, glory, I saw my mother. And my love is a poor boy on a borrowed bicycle that only got one stick of candy in his life, poor boy. Oh Lord, sweet Lord, let me rest myself a little while. I feel so wanting. I feel so bad a-wanting.

Wileem put the other one to bed early after supper but it was already dark then because of the gathering storm.

"Goodnight, Sister. Goodnight."

Even in the darkness, the quick eyes followed Wileem out of the room, but there was no expression on the other one's face and she didn't say anything.

Jarvie came when the new moon crept out into an open patch of sky and shivered there thin and nervously fingering the house and the pear tree. He came skulking up the hill through the grass, drunk and excited and carrying whiskey in his pocket.

Wileem let him into the kitchen but didn't turn on the light so that the moon shone on the linoleum floor and there was the smell of bacon grease and coffee and, now, of whiskey.

"Ol' battleax gone?"

"Aunt's singing down yonder, don't you hear?"

They spoke in whispers and then stood close together, their warm breath beating out into the rain-tight air and listened to the voices weeping like river waves at the foot of the hill.

"Pretty girl."

"Yes," Wileem panted. "Yes, yes."

Then she pulled away from him and ran across the moonlit floor in her bare feet and stood leaning her back against the table and breathing oddly and laughing.

"No. Say it first. Say you love me to pieces. Say it."

"God, Wileem. God."

"Jarvie, say it."

"Don't tease, girl. I love you, Wileem."

He ran after her and touched her warm bare arms but she said, "Boy on a bicycle, say it again. Talk to me."

"Talk? You're crazy. Come here."

"Show me the pistol first. You promised."

"Oh, Wileem."

"Show me."

"Here."

It was a tiny silver twink in the moonlight. She took it and put her cheek against it.

"A boy's a man when he gets him a gun. Say you love me. No, first say it."

She laughed again. She laid the gun on the table and ran again and he caught her in a shadow. Suddenly they sprang apart and stood staring and choking on their breath.

The other one stood in the kitchen in a patch of moonlight. She wore only a white chemise, very short, and her strange sharp face was expressionless in the midst of her red hair but her bright eyes looked for Wileem.

"Sister, go back to bed. Go back upstairs," Wileem gasped.

Jarvie began to laugh. A crazy whiskey laugh that choked the kitchen and strangled the gospel singing and dried up the river. He began to move toward Wileem again.

"Jarvie, wait."

He came on and the other one stood still and watched him but didn't say anything.

"Jarvie, wait," Wileem's voice was deep and throaty and dangerous.

The other one had picked up the pistol from the table. As Jarvie reached out to touch Wileem the other one shot him down with his own pistol. He fell hard. He flopped on the linoleum floor but scrambled up again almost at once, gone cold sober, swearing and bleeding. He grabbed the pistol from the other one's hand and jammed it into his pocket.

"Every goddamn female bitch in this stinking house is crazy as a fuckin' bedbug," he shouted, holding his arm. He took another frowning stare around the kitchen and walked to the door where he said, "So long, Honeybabe. So long to you, your nutty sister and your half-wit aunt. You are too much for me."

He slammed the door so hard it hurt Wileem's teeth. She followed him as fast as she could, but when she opened the door and looked, he was gone out of sight. She stared down at her bare feet which were warm and sticky with blood.

She turned back and saw the other one still standing there. Wileem stuck out her tongue.

"What'd you want to go and do that for, you silly thing? You block of wood? I purely hate you!" she hissed out harsh as fingernails scratching stone.

Scowling, Wileem turned and went upstairs.

Wileem stood by the bedroom window. She didn't even turn around when the other one came up and got back into bed. She kept standing there on into the night listening to the gospel singing sob along the old river and float up where the hill waited for rain. She watched for Jarvie to come back until the moon set.

When she did climb into bed, the room was too dark for Wileem to make out the other one's face lying expressionless in the middle of her tangled red hair or to see her eyes which were still open or the tears that rolled down her cheeks without a sign of stopping.

Loaves and Fishes

When it was time to start supper, she began to listen for Kenny's step on the road.

Aileen, who liked to keep her busy, said, "Help me dust the room, Mother. Have you forgotten my party?"

A mobile, five fishes made of colored paper stretched on wooden frames, hung on a black thread from the chandelier. The air stirred by Aileen passing made the fishes wheel and turn.

"Those fishes never touch each other," Catherine said. "Never once."

It was true. She had watched the mobile all winter and when a breeze blew, the fishes darted back and forth but never touched. The red one never touched the blue one. The green one never touched the gold or the black.

Catherine took up the dust cloth, gazing about her. A sofa had come where her bedstead usually stood and there was an orange rug.

"Why, where's the bed?" she asked reasonably.

"But, Mother, you remember. I bought the sofa three years ago."

"Yes," she said. "Oh, yes."

She trailed the cloth along the table. Aileen liked to move the furniture, of course.

"I got new slip covers for the party, Mother. I'll tell you since you haven't noticed. They're awfully nice material. The clerk said I had a knack for picking first class goods."

But Catherine was looking out of the window. Kenny would swing around the bend in the road any time now. Like as not he'd lift her off her feet as he always did when he hugged her 'hello.'

"I've invited Ida Belle for you," Aileen remarked, "and Bess, of course, and Jewel. And then some of my bridge club gang. They've none of them seen the house since I painted the downstairs. Did you see the mirror I got for the hall? It's oval. A bone-white frame. Go look at it."

Aileen was a girl who liked nice things. And the room was tasteful, surely.

When Catherine got into the hall it seemed to her she'd come to open the front door. She could scarcely manage to swing it since the hinges were changed. She stood on the door sill, looking out past the drive. She had thought Kenny would be standing there waiting to be let in.

"Mother, close the door."

It was cold outside, frosty and bright. A good day for walking. Kenny would be walking out from the edge of Flytown. He'd come over the hills with a bunch of the children hanging onto him as they always did.

"Close the door and come sit down," Aileen said. "You'll tire yourself out and you won't enjoy the party when I'm giving it just to please you."

Catherine sat in the rocker and her daughter pushed a bundle under her fingers. She lifted it up, fumbling with the skeins of thread.

"That's a dish towel," she remarked when she had looked at it.

The guests began to ring the bell at four.

"You have a flair for decorating," they cried to Aileen as they stared about. "But then you've got the money to get nice things."

They had tea. The daughter used her Wedgwood pot.

"I thought your coming might liven Mother up," Aileen said. Her fingers on the pot were quick and dexterous.

"Catherine's lost flesh since she's went into her seventies," Ida Belle observed. "She's a little bit of a mite like her sister was before she died of a stroke, God rest her."

"Goes on with her embroidery, though," said Jewel.

"I urge her at it. Otherwise she'd just sit."

"You're a wonder with her, Aileen," the women said. "It's a marvel how you look after your mother. You handle her so well. And then you keep her looking so nice."

Catherine, far off, looked down at Catherine drinking tea. She hung like a bat in a corner of the room, listening.

"She must bless the day she had you, Aileen, the care you take of her."

"No. Oh, no. It's always Kenny with her, you see."

"Well."

"A manchild," Ida Belle said indulgently.

Yes, but over and above that, Aileen told them, frowning, there was always some sort of secret between the two of them that left her out. And all that hugging. Aileen was undemonstrative like her papa.

"And Kenny being the first born," the ladies said.

They began to speak of their children and of their grandchildren. Their voices waxed lush, bloomed tropically up out of their throats.

Catherine swam above them in another element, similar to water only thinner and quicker moving, like a stream of clear light. She was especially fond of the ceiling. The free Catherine swam in among the paper fishes and touched them: the red, and the blue, the gold, the green and the black, each one, gently. The talk of the ladies about their children moved up around her, spreading ripples.

In a fey mood, the free Catherine peeped over the chandelier, down through the fish shapes at the ladies sitting below supporting their great crystal wombs delicately on their knees. Inside the wombs she could see the children moving about.

"Mother."

"Well then, what?"

"Will you come with us, Mother? The girls want a tour. They want to see the painting I've done."

"All right."

"Now, I did the kitchen in a clear red. What do you think? I refinished the table. That's the one Mother had when we were children, you know. It's worth a nice figure by now, I shouldn't wonder. I'll open it out. I keep it folded. We never sit down to eat any more. Almost never. Arch eats downtown or at Lions', Reba's middle name is 'go' and I'm always on the run."

"Yes, and Kenny sits there, opposite, against the wall," Catherine burst out so suddenly that everyone fell silent. "Before he'd take his place, he used to go around the table and give everyone of us a kiss, do you remember, Aileen? When he was little? And even now he's grown up he does that sometimes."

"Mother, you're holding up our tour," Aileen said.

"Ah well," Catherine said, surprised.

When they came to Reba's room, they found the door locked. Aileen tapped on one of the upper panels.

"Reba," she said. "May I come in? I want to show the ladies your room. Unlock the door, dearie."

"No," Reba said, indistinctly.

"Reba?"

"No. No. No."

"She's crying in there, I think," Aileen said, backing away. "A broken romance, I suspect. She never tells me, of course. Ha. Ha."

"Teen-agers!" the ladies murmured, smirking.

The visitors left at five-thirty. Catherine stood on the front stoop, waving. The cold bright air spanked her cheeks and pulled at her hair. It brought her wider awake.

"Look at the road!" she said to Aileen.

"Yes."

"Why, it's wrong. It goes down the hill instead of along the ridge. It's been torn up and changed."

"I know about the road, Mother," Aileen said. "Please come in and close the door. You'll catch cold."

Her hands fumbled with the knob. There now. She had suspected for days her daughter was up to something. Aileen was a good girl but she sometimes told lies. Catherine had caught her telling lies more than once.

"I'll just walk out to the road and see how it's been shifted," she said. She was afraid Kenny couldn't find his way home.

"Mother, step in here."

She stood still. Her daughter's tone suddenly caught her up short. A coldness that was not the wind touched her. There was a danger here. Her memory stirred, groping back.

The door closed smartly and all was as it had been except that Catherine was left puzzling over that glimpse of darkness like the gaping maw of a wolf waiting for her.

"Sit down, Mother."

Miraculously, there was the dish towel again in her fingers. She picked at it, irritably.

"Your new dress looked well, Mother. Did you hear Ida Belle mention it?"

She peered down at herself.

"The color suits you. I got blue because it compliments your complexion. That's a fifty dollar dress, Mother."

"I like pockets."

"They don't make dresses with pockets now."

"When you were small," she told Aileen, "I'd put a gum drop in each of my pockets and here'd come little hands searching for them. That's how I'd get a hug out of you! What do you think of that?"

"Your hair has come loose, Mother. Don't you feel it on your neck? I wonder: should we try a permanent? It's gotten so thin and fine the comb will barely catch it."

"When I first married," said Catherine, "my hair was thick as your own and so long I could sit on it. Do you mind how your papa used to have to brush out the tangles when my arms got tired?"

"I remember he made you bob your hair because he said it was a nuisance," the daughter cut in abruptly. "That was the summer he took me downtown with him to Swirl, Incorporated, and taught me to keep his books. He said I knew the value of a dollar and Kenny didn't because Kenny wouldn't sell washers but went to teaching in that ratty Flytown school. Papa had a sharp eye for business, didn't he?"

"How so?"

"Why, Kenny never had a nickle and I've pushed Arch up to vice-president in the company. We're in the five figure bracket, Mother.

"I'm going to shower and dress, now," the daughter went on. "My lodge meets tonight. Do you remember my telling you I was elected matriarch this year?"

Left alone, Catherine lifted the curtain. The shadows of trees lay across the road dark as streaks of old blood.

Almost at once she heard him outside on the stoop. She was certain of it. She stepped across the carpet and dragged the door open. A tall man who was not Kenny stood outside.

Carrying a carton of beer packed in tin cans, he walked quickly through the living room and out into the kitchen, where she could hear him opening and closing drawers.

When Aileen came back wearing a different dress, she said,

"Ah, Mother. There you stand with the door open again and the house cold as a tomb."

"He came in."

"Who? Why, there's mud on my carpet! Who came in?"

A can clattered into the sink in the kitchen.

"Who's there?" the daughter called out. She bent over, picking at the rug with her fingernail.

"Me. I'm here," the man's voice answered, muffled by the walls.

"Arch?"

"It is. Yes."

"Are you home so early? You shouldn't leave work so early, I don't think."

"Why not?"

"It doesn't look well, you know. You get a slacker's image, sort of. They notice who ducks out and who stays."

"I was tired."

"Still."

Aileen at forty was a tall woman with a large head and calculating brown eyes. She spoke as always with a studied distinctness as if her words were coins she was counting out.

"Did you pick up the suit I ordered for you?" she called.

"What?" he said.

She repeated herself but he had the water running in the sink and only said again, "What? What?"

Then he could be heard walking off to another part of the house.

Catherine thought suddenly that she would bake bread against Kenny's coming. She went into the kitchen and tied on her apron. Lifting down the blue canister, she stuck her fingers into the flour. It felt warm as if the wheat had kept the rich heat of the sun through cutting and grinding.

But the rolling pin was gone out of the drawer and the bread pans were lost and the oven raised high up and unnatural. She could in no way light it.

"Well, Mother, what are you about?" her daughter asked, wondering.

"I'd thought I'd make bread."

"Bread!" cried Aileen.

"I thought to help the supper out."

"You don't need to fuss in the kitchen, Mother," Aileen said, taking away the canister. "I buy my bread at the bakery. Besides no one will have time to eat much tonight. Now go and sit while I clean up the flour. Has Reba come out of her room yet?"

"No."

"Reba!" Aileen raised her voice. "I want you to fix your grandma a tray. Do you hear me, Reba?"

"What?" the granddaughter spoke through her closed door.

"And don't forget band practice tonight, deary. You'd better get on the stick. If you think you aren't going, think again, miss. Your dad and I didn't lay out all that money on a flute and lessons for no reason. Besides all the work I do for Band Boosters. We're taking Joanne and Harry to the game on purpose to watch you Friday night. Come on out now, Reba."

Catherine panted, short of breath. Aileen's voice filled the kitchen, using up all the air.

"I can't find my bread pans," Catherine said.

She paced the floor almost on the point of tears. The kitchen was so strange, after all. She stood in the middle of the room.

"You can't make bread, Mother. There simply is not time."

"I baked all our bread when you children were small," Catherine said. "How Kenny liked the warm heels with honey on! He said they were good as kisses from your sweetheart!"

"Come sit in the living room, Mother," Aileen said. "Let me help you take off your apron. It's all over flour. You know, people don't wear cobbler's aprons any more."

"It's got pockets."

"Nevertheless, take it off. I want to show the ladies coming to pick me up how well your new dress suits you."

But she was disturbed and resisted her daughter's fingers on her clothes. Kenny should be home by now. Could there be trouble at the school again? Perhaps he wouldn't come until morning. He'd been away all night before. But then he'd come home so tired. He'd leave his breakfast lay. 'Those poor children,' he'd say. 'Oh, Mama, those poor mites.' He meant the ones in Flytown. The ones without shoes.

"Look at the dish towel, Mother. See?" her daughter said. "I've brought all the thread. Now you're ready to begin on the red daisies, aren't you?"

She looked at the thread but the colors were dim as if a film was over them. She glanced up at the paper fishes and even they had a grey look so she could hardly sort out the red from the blue or the gold from the green or black. Her heart hurt her because everything was turned dull: the wallpaper, the curtains, the slipcovers, even Aileen's face.

Then the footsteps rang out clear on the frosty road. She felt each one sharp and plain: there, there, there. In the very coursing of her blood she detected them slyly with an uncanny certainty of perception more acute than hearing.

"What is it, Mother?" Her daughter was alarmed, for Catherine stood suddenly, scattering the rug with skeins of thread.

"Hark!" she said. "Hark!"

She crossed the room and opened the door. The wind that blew into her face was full of sparkles of ice. It pulled her hair loose from its comb and made her eyes smart.

She stood aghast, for the doorway was filled with unknown people: women with handsome coats and high boots and hair curling astoundingly about their faces.

They came wantonly into the house crying out in high voices. She, backing away, peered at them as they pushed into the hall. Not a one offered to shake hands. Certainly they were strange and the hall itself was surpassingly strange and the room beyond with its smart sofa and its flowered chairs.

"Where is this?" she said, staring about. "Where is this?"

Her daughter came quickly to her side.

"I'm not at home," she said to Aileen, the pitch rising on each syllable until the memory of the last word hung shockingly high in the silence that followed.

"That's all right, Mother," Aileen said, but her voice was like a warning.

Catherine pressed on, although she was afraid.

"Where am I!" she asked. "Where? Where?"

"You're at my house, Mother."

"No," she said. But she knew exactly where she was now. On

the edge of Tapp City. Miles from the home place.

The women were struck dumb with wonder, listening. The daughter's face was white and her eyes glittered.

"I want to go home," Catherine called out louder than was necessary, for the women caught their breath. "Kenny is waiting for me at home."

The danger moved nearer at once. Its black maw opened, letting out a breath that stank. She twisted her hands together as if she would wring blood from the knuckles. She trembled, knowing the danger was upon her.

Aileen moved forward so that she stood facing her.

"Listen closely, Mother," Aileen said. "I've told you this before. Kenny has been dead for twenty years. He was hanged by vigilantes for trying to bring the Flytown children into the Sardis school. Surely you remember. You laid him out yourself. He's buried in the cemetery by the Church of the Blessed in Sardis. Kenny is gone, Mother. He's gone."

The women were poised, still as statues, not daring to move.

"Why don't you go to your room and rest?" Aileen said. She spoke with great firmness, so that Catherine went and lay down on her bed. But after the house grew quiet she got up again, knowing as she did that Aileen told lies.

She hurried to put on her shoes but the laces snarled and she kicked them away and donned her slippers instead.

When she was ready, she tiptoed through the living room, tugged open the stubborn front door and stepped out of the house.

It was dark bitter night outside. The smell of snow was on the wind. The street lamps were blurred as if they shone through spun sugar. She missed the walk and struck off across the lawn staring at the cold shadows under the bushes. All of the houses were ash-colored like burnt-out logs.

When she reached the road, she walked along it toward the home place. After she had walked a while she sat down to rest on the road's edge. Her hair was flying loose, and she tried to fasten it with the comb but it wouldn't be caught. She found she had lost one slipper and while she was searching for it, she fell asleep.

She slept a long time through a forgetfulness like death that was yet filled with fleeting sensation. She identified a vivid presence of light and warmth so intimate and personal yet so vast that she supposed herself by turns to be beside a glowing hearth and then upon the rim of a planet that was burning.

When she arose struggling through sleep to wakefulness the warmth transmuted itself into Kenny's arms, lifting her.

Opening her eyes, Catherine saw that the porch lights were turned on in front of all the houses along the road and that people were running over the lawns. They came toward her from all directions.

"There you are!" they cried. "What are you doing out here? Whyever did you leave the house on such a night?"

The free Catherine, quite content to stay lifted up in Kenny's arms, looked down for a long time on the people shouting at the Catherine below before she understood they would get no answers from her any more.

The Hollyhock Doll

Out where the hollyhocks bloomed tall in the orchard, Dorcas lay full-length in the long wet grass. Little by little as she waited, the crickets and the tree toads, the screech owl and the whippoorwill started up again. But not the frogs in the pond. They were more heedful.

Dorcas rested her chin on the good-smelling earth and her hair, wet from the dew, hung down over the bank as if it grew there amongst the rushes. When at last the frogs started in, a thousand different frog voices came spreading up from the water.

The little noises came into her head and filled it and into her whole self and filled that. Fuller and fuller. She would burst open and her ragged ends spread out there and there over the evening sky. In the house, the baby slept.

In town, Corene switched on the lamp by the couch, intending to read there. The night was ugly with the heat. She stood like a stout resentful kewpie, pouting at the couch.

"God, even after all this time, I can't sit there," she said. "Because that's where he died. On that very spot. On a Saturday night. Eating popcorn, for godsake, popcorn!"

She stalked across the room and plopped her bottom down into the yellow plastic chair. She pulled a hankie from up her sleeve and wiped her upper lip.

"Corene, is that you? Is that you in the parlour? Corene? It's ten o'clock. Have you looked at a clock lately? My alarm clock says it's ten minutes after ten o'clock."

"Mama, for christsake. I'll come to bed in a minute, Mama."

"I can't sleep with you kerwhanging around the parlour all hours. I lay here on my back day and night and it — ."

"I know you lay there on your back, Mama."

Corene had picked up the newspaper from the yellow footstool and was turning the pages over slowly.

"I'm a woman eighty-four years old, I want you to — ."

"I know you're eighty-fo — ."

"Eighty-four years old. And what have I got to show. A paralyzed back and an ungrateful daughter, that's you, Corene, and not one grandchild."

Corene dropped the paper like a sheet of hot tin and sat staring straight before her stuffing her hankie up her sleeve.

"I'm going up to the Cutrate," she said.

"It's ten minutes after ten o'clock at night."

Corene got up out of the yellow chair and stood in front of a small round mirror hanging over the sewing machine. She licked her little finger and ran it twice over one eyebrow.

"Bring me a glass of water to put my teeth in," her mother said.

Corene went into the kitchen which was very small and curtained in blue plastic ruffles, and turned on the spigot. She got two glasses from the cupboard, filled both. She set one on the sink board and used the other to gargle with after adding a few drops of amber liquid from a bottle. She gargled without tilting back her head much and with one arm propped akimbo.

On her way out of the kitchen with the other glass of water, she picked up a small brown paper bag from the kitchen table. In the parlour she set the glass of water down on the sewing machine, opened the bag and took out three pink paper geraniums all wound on the same green stem. Staring into the mirror she pinned the geraniums onto the front of her dress.

"Here I can't move up off this bed and I got to ask twenty times before anybody will fetch in one glass of water to put my teeth in."

"Mama I got two hands and two feet, for your information. What happened to the glass to put your teeth in I brought you at noon?"

Corene carried the water into the bedroom and set it on the dresser.

"My God, Mama, what do you absolutely have to have these ferns just about on top of your bed for? They drip on the rug and they smell like rotten apples."

She moved two large ferns in red clay pots off the night stand, put them on the window ledge and put the glass of water on the night stand. The bedroom was very small, done in paper with ovals of George and Martha Washington. The old woman, propped up in a hospital bed, looked quite dead except for her bright restless eyes. She had on a purple dress.

"Them ferns is my company."

"What happened to the water glass I brought you at noon?"

"Dr. Deleweese was here. While you was to the store. He gave me a white pill to take. It was long, like this. About this long. He took and broke it in two and poured the insides into the glass and it phizzed up. So he said, drink it."

"Oh."

"He stayed half an hour."

"What'd he say?"

Corene picked up the alarm clock from the dresser, turned it around to look at it, wound it two turns and set it back.

"He said he still can't tell what's wrong with me. Not exactly, he said. Some nerve trouble. He can't cure it until he finds out exactly, he said. He thought maybe this pill I took will help it. Maybe I'll be able to get up tomorrow. He said he wasn't sure. Here, take my teeth."

Corene took them and put them into the water glass.

"Mouthwash. You smell like mouthwash," her mother said.

Corene watched the bubbles rise from the dentures.

"You ain't used mouthwash since George went, rest him. I said you smell like mouthwash."

"I heard you, Mama."

The old woman turned her head toward Corene quickly and jerkily like a hen.

"What's that you got pinned on you?"

"It happens that I have got a paper geranium pinned on."

"I never seen it before, that geranium."

"I'm going to walk up to the Cutrate."

"It's ten-thirty o'clock, Corene."

"Mama, I know it's ten-thirty o'clock. You want I should crank your bed?"

"Yes, crank it."

By the time Corene had cranked down the bed and switched off the light, the old woman had begun to snore faintly through her mouth.

Corene crossed the parlour and went into her own bedroom. She came out with a subtle and deep expression, stuffing a fresh handkerchief up her sleeve. The handkerchief was bordered with yellow pansies.

Out on the porch, it was hotter even than inside. Before she stepped off the porch she looked for and spotted the end of Mr. Wilmot's cigar. Her lips loosened down into a secretive line. She stood there a moment straightening the geranium.

Helter-skelter screeching and careening a car burst onto the quiet street. The car radio was playing a blue yodle tuned up louder than a shout. The car, an eight-year-old sedan, ran up over the curb, stopped, stood rocking from side to side. The man in the car stripped the gears, pulled off back onto the street and went on down town in a hurry.

Corene blanched and shook all over. Mr. Wilmot hurried off of his porch and down the sidewalk and stared after the car. He met Corene when he walked back.

"Did you see that?" he shouted. "Was you watching that? How's your mama?"

"Mr. Wilmot, I told you at half past seven o'clock this evening when I went to the Frozen Food Locker, Mama is the same. She's the same."

"Did you see Edan Allen? That was Edan Allen in that car."

"What on God's earth was wrong with him?"

"He's drinking beer. He's been riding around town in his car since four o'clock drinking store bought beer. He's been throwing out the bottles. He almost hit the Kennerson girl, the cross-eyed one, with a bottle in front of the Pure Oil. She was mad."

Mr. Wilmot took his cigar out of his mouth. He looked at the pink paper geraniums.

"Edan Allen never used to drink much," Mr. Wilmot remarked. "Maybe he is worried about Dorcas finding out."

Corene stared at the red apoplectic splotches on Mr. Wilmot's face.

"Mr. Wilmot, what would Dorcas care if he drinks beer? A half-Indian, for godsake, or gypsy or half whatever she is. And no sense at all, let me hasten to add."

"I mean he drinks beer because he's worried Dorcas will find out about his town girl. I meant to say. Half-Indian or not half-Indian, Dorcas's still his wife.

Corene began to move on down the sidewalk. Mr. Wilmot followed her a few more steps.

"Or more likely it's his conscience, you know, because she don't suspect."

Corene kept walking. Out of the corner of her eye she saw Mr. Wilmot turn back.

"Mr. Wilmot, I'd appreciate you keeping a eye on Mama while I run to the Cutrate," she said over her shoulder without stopping.

She did not hear him answer. The roots of the trees had pushed up the sidewalk all along the way in front of her. Up and down the street people were sitting on their porches tilted back in kitchen chairs or creaking to and fro in chain-hung swings or squatting on the top step. A few of them called down asking Corene how her mother was.

Corene remarked to the last person who asked about her mother that Mr. Wilmot was driving her mother out of her mind because "he talks and talks and thinks he *knows* so much, for godsake!"

Downtown the street lights were fluttering behind clouds of bugs. Most of the stores were closed. A row of old men sat on a bench in front of the post office, some of them dozing.

Corene went into the drugstore. She ordered a strawberry ice cream cone. A long-bladed ceiling fan stirred the hot air and pushed it down on top of her head. She took her cone and sat down in a booth at the back of the store. The varnish on the seat was sticky with the heat. She ate the ice cream cone so slowly it melted and ran down over her fingers.

She watched the door. A fly ran down her arm on quick feet.

The counter girl was reading a confession magazine. Corene got up and bought a magazine and returned to the booth. She sat turning over the pages slowly staring at the cigarette ads and the colored recipe illustrations.

After she had been in the booth almost an hour the door opened. Corene half stood up, stared, and sat back down on the sticky varnish. It was the counter girl's boy friend. He straddled a stool with his elbows on the counter. The girl put her head close to his, leaning across the chewing gum display. They whispered.

Corene glanced at the door. No one came in. She turned over five magazine pages rapidly. The counter girl and her boy friend giggled. They stole glances at Corene.

The wall of the booth was riddled with penciled initials. There was a heart drawn with lipstick. An obscene word had been cut in it with a knife. At a quarter to twelve, Corene got up and walked out of the drugstore. She stood with small tears of disappointment in her eyes, looking up and down the street. The lights in the drugstore went out.

After a while the counter girl and her boy friend came out. The girl locked up the door and they went off down the street together.

Corene looked up and down the street and started to walk home. She had only gone a few steps when she heard a great crash and stopped to see what it was.

At twelve fifteen the eight-year-old sedan that had been careening around town all evening ran through the plate glass window of the Farmers' Savings Bank. It set off the bank's alarm system.

Everybody in town woke up. Pretty soon most of them got dressed and went down to the bank to see what was going on. The car radiator was smashed clear into the side of the teller's cage. The truck and spinning rear wheels of the car were still out on the sidewalk.

Edan Allen, a husky sunburned fellow with ears flat to his head, was sitting behind the shattered windshield bleeding down onto the runningboard. He appeared to be studying a sign on the bank wall in front of him that said, "$10,000 maximum insurance for each depositor. Member Federal Deposit Insurance Corporation." He was, however, dead. His chest had been crushed by the steering wheel.

The bank's alarm kept on ringing. It began to get on people's nerves. No one knew how to shut it off. They sent a boy to wake up the head teller who knew how to shut it off.

They sent another boy out into the country to fetch Edan's wife, Dorcas. The town marshal and the volunteer fire department tried to get Edan out of the car but he was pinned in. They all worked hard at it, sweating their shirts black because of the intense heat while the rest of the people, with more coming all the time, stood around and gave advice on how to get the job done.

It was a wonder the boy found Dorcas at all. The Allen shack was wide open, windows and doors, but dark and no one was there. Dorcas was still mooning down by the frog pond.

The boy stood undecided and fidgeting for ten minutes at the end of which time Dorcas walked up out of the orchard carrying six hollyhock stalks and whistling.

"Is that you, Dorcas Ann?"

"Yes, it's me."

She walked up to the boy, peered into his face, then detoured around him to the well and untied the rope. She put her palm against the wooden spindle and let the rope spin out down the well. After a bit there was a cool settling sound far down.

Dorcas laid the hollyhocks on the grass and wound up the wet rope, grunting as the turning got harder.

"You are standing on my petunia flower bed," she remarked to the boy. "In the middle."

He stepped backward. The petunias were growing in the hole of a rubber tire laid on the ground. After a while the tin cylinder came out of the well. It dripped and sweated ice cold water. Dorcas set it down in an enamel pail and the water poured into the pail.

She took the cylinder and picked up the hollyhocks and stuck them down into the bucket.

"Now is when you tell me what you want," she said.

The boy watched her dry her hands on her thighs before he said anything.

"They want you should come into town."

"What in Sweet Jesus for?"

"Edan took and run through the plate glass window of the Farmer's Bank building with his car. Just now."

Dorcas made a soft wordless sound.

"Is he kilt?"

"I don't know. I come straight off here. They sent me to fetch you down there. To see about it."

Dorcas looked at her feet.

"I got to put some shoes on and get the baby."

She went into the shack and returned at once wearing a pair of men's work shoes with the baby straddling her hip still asleep. The boy and Dorcas walked to town in silence through hot moonlight. They went single file down the dirt road. The baby's hair reflected the moon color in a mist around its head. It slept all the way.

When Dorcas and the boy reached the Pure Oil gasoline station, they could hear the bank alarm still ringing. The crowd around the bank was so thick they couldn't see the car until they pushed in and touched the rear bumper.

The people, seeing who it was, fanned back a little. Dorcas stood beside the car and peered into the front seat where the volunteer fire department was still trying to get Edan out. They had a blowtorch and were using it on the dashboard.

Dorcas looked at Edan. Then she looked up and down the faces of the men and women standing around the car. Her face had a closed pondering expression.

"I wish to God they'd shut off that bell," said a woman.

One of the volunteer firemen who had been lying on his back in the front seat came out and used his shirt tail to wipe his face.

"It's going to take six hours to cut him loose," he said staring in his hand at the tail of his shirt. "Six goddamn hours. Anyway."

The baby stirred on Dorcas's hip and whimpered softly like an animal.

"That pore lamb don't know what it's lost," a woman said.

Dorcas turned around and looked at the woman solemnly.

"That's God's truth," she said, impressed. "That's God's own truth."

At four-thirty in the morning the volunteer fire department told Dorcas to go on home. By that time most of the people were back in bed asleep. The head teller had finally been located and had turned the alarm off. It was very quiet after that.

They had rolled the sedan out of the bank and into the street where glass fell off of the running boards into the gutter. Dorcas sat down on somebody's kitchen chair and the baby went to sleep over her knees bottom side up.

When they told her to go along home, Dorcas got up and walked around the car until they finally got Edan out of it and carried him off. Then she started home through the fields. The baby, a boy about one year old, woke and wanted down. The sun was not up yet but it was hot. Dorcas took off the baby's nightdress and let him run away over the ground.

He wandered farther and farther ahead until she began to jog after him into the weakening dark. She caught him near the shack on the banks of a small muddy creek. She picked him up. The baby blew little warm breaths against her cheek while he wiggled to get down again. His very soft hair fell across her mouth.

Dorcas set the baby down with his feet in the cool running water. He looked at her with never a smile, his brown eyes wondering. He walked up out of the water studying his feet. He fell asleep at once when Dorcas put him to bed inside the shack.

Dorcas went into the front room where she looked into one or two closets and lifted a black stone crock from the table and set it down again. She took off her shoes on the front stoop and walked out into the yard. The sunrise wind was in the pear tree, the grass, the bushes.

The sky lightened slowly. The orchard trees shook loose of their shadow and every single rock and grass and piece of chicken dung in the yard was plain. How stiff and hard her face felt! How the lines of it hurt her! But she had no other way to hold it at this minute.

She turned back into the shack. In the kitchen she pushed a pot of cold boiled coffee over a burner. From a tumbler on the table she counted out three, four, five toothpicks and put them into her pocket. She got a small sharp kitchen knife from the cupboard and carried it out the back door.

By the well the hollyhocks stood propped in a pail of water leaning against the well cover. Dorcas picked out a red hollyhock with three big flowers and took it over to the back steps and sat down. She was very careful. She took off the flowers, each one without tearing, and a bud and arranged them in a pile at her feet.

She stuck one toothpick through all the flowers and the top of it into the bud. She made arms and legs out of the other toothpicks, poking them into the flowers. She cut a face on the bud.

Dorcas carried the doll into the kitchen and poured out a cup of coffee and set it on the table. She took the doll on into the baby's room and set its flower skirt over one knob on the foot of the crib where the baby would see it when he woke up.

Back in the kitchen she sat down at the table and drank out of the cup. On the stove, the coffee bubbled up the sides of the pot and out over the top. After she had drunk up the coffee in the cup, she hadn't a thing in the world to do until the baby woke up and it was time for breakfast.

Corene got home at about two o'clock in the morning. A few people were still hurrying off downtown. One or two heads stuck out of second story windows. The bank alarm system had just stopped ringing.

She climbed the steps to her porch slowly with her back slightly bent over like a person either tired or old.

"Hey, Corene."

Corene stopped on the porch and turned around.

"Mrs. Wilmot? What in the wide world are you standing over here in our bushes for at two A.M. in the morning, Mrs. Wilmot?"

"I was watching for you to come home, dear, because I wanted to rest your mind on the score of your mama. Floyd and me has been taking turns downtown and watching your mama. At the moment she's sleeping like a baby, bless her. Floyd is downtown."

"Well, thanks until you're better paid, Mrs. Wilmot, I'm sure."

"You're welcome. It's so quiet, ain't it? I mean now."

"Yes. That goddamned Ralph Lester was watching the TV all the way over at his brother-in-law's, the one that's on social security, and they just about gave up finding him to shut the alarm off."

"Well, I'm glad he come and done it."

The street was in heavy shadow. The dark lay concentrated and palpable in the foliage of the trees. The two o'clock quiet was so noticeable it seemed everybody in town was sitting around their houses holding their breaths for fear or curiosity or wonderment.

Mrs. Wilmot cleared her throat, started to speak, and cleared it again.

"Well, I guess I'll go downtown, dear, see can I locate Floyd. But, say, I want you to know, Corene, we feel so sorry for you."

"Mrs. Wilmot, a lots of people, even in this very town, has got their bedfast mothers to look after, or their bedfast fathers. I—."

"I don't mean your mama, dear. I mean Edan."

Mrs. Wilmot gave Corene's arm three short pats above the elbow. Corene turned around and walked across the front porch to the screen door. Mrs. Wilmot walked out onto the sidewalk and on down toward the center of town, bobbing up and down over the sidewalk pushed up by tree roots.

Corene stepped into the parlour and switched on the two reading lamps. She picked up the newspaper from the yellow footstool, folded it, laid it back down and sat down heavily on the couch.

"Corene, is that you?"

"Yes, Mama. Go back to sleep."

"What's wrong? What's wrong with everybody tonight? I seen the Wilmot's lights on over past twelve o'clock. They always go to bed at nine. And here you're roaming around the parlour at half after two in the morning."

"It's the heat, Mama, is all. I expect people can't sleep when it's so—."

"No sir. There's something going on, Corene. Come in here. I want you to crank the bed. I want to know what all is going on. I heard a noise like a—well sort of a buzz. And I seen some people all going downtown. A lot earlier. Here I am on this bed struck down with nerve trouble and nobody will even so much as tell me—."

"You ain't struck down with nerve trouble, Mama. You had a stroke, for godsake."

Corene picked up the newspaper and fanned her face with it vigorously.

After a while her mother said, "Did you say stroke, Corene?"

"Well, yes. The fact of the matter is, Mama, you've had two. It just once in a while seems to me a woman of eighty-four years old would know when she's had two strokes."

There came a pause between them in the conversation. It grew into a silence. The silence spread from the two women until it held the whole house.

Corene laid the newspaper across her lap and blew her nose on her handkerchief. When she stood up the paper fell off her lap to the floor. She let it lay.

She switched off the two reading lamps, walking heavily across the floor from one to the other. She stood in the dark stuffing the ball of her handkerchief up under her right sleeve. Her mother began to snore gently from the other room.

Corene wondered when, for godsake, the Wilmots were going to come home from downtown and turn their back porch light off and go to bed.

The Pinning

Adrian's hands were his main assets. He had to admit it. His fingers were long and quick. He was going to be great shakes at tying surgeon's knots.

His other asset was his hair. It was red and curly as corkscrews. And girls liked it.

He stopped beside a spiffy little foreign-make with a side mirror, put his books on the fender and fished out his comb. Might as well look good for Katie. What the hell?

Bending over to look in the mirror he gave the car the once-over. Four on the floor. Bucket seats. More room inside than he'd expected.

Two clowns came walking up behind him. Adrian picked up his books and rubbed off the fender with two fingers.

"What's the mileage she makes you, buddy?" one of the clowns said to Adrian.

"Thirty. Twenty-seven once when I eased her to Omaha."

"Very, very nice."

They bent over and looked in the window. Walking away, Adrian said, "I can get two adults, two kids, four suitcases and a dog in there. If it's a pretty small dog."

After that everything looked top drawer. Why worry? Nuts even to the Katie business. The most she could do was slap his face.

Here's what he liked to do: a slow eye-lift, roofs, chimneys, tree tops, hills, sky, Bingo! He stopped at a curb and gave the traffic light the Evil Eye but it stayed red.

Adrian used the time to tuck his collar flaps under his sweater. He took a look at the reflection of his neck in the glass door of a telephone booth.

You know Adrian Steffens. Brilliant mind. Immaculate dresser. Up and comer. He leaned a little forward watching the reflections of two girls with tennis rackets but they didn't look back after they passed him.

The time for meeting Katie was creeping up on him. Here was the ticket: if the letter was there he'd give her the word. Simple break. Clean as bone.

Only he hoped she wouldn't have on the blue scarf, that damn scarf that made her look like the Virgin Mary. She'd worn it tied over her hair the night of the last dance at the high school. Why the hell should he remember that? Marilyn had a diamond clip in hers. That he should remember.

Everything'd go slick as oil. If only she didn't have on that blue scarf and didn't pull any of those nutty tricks of hers like lifting up the back of her hair and putting his hand on her neck underneath where it was warm and damp.

If the letter wasn't there, he'd just wait a while. Nobody knew. Except maybe his mom. He couldn't help slipping her a hint or two. She'd be so set up.

This business was too hard on the nerves. His grades were going to the devil. And he'd jerked another hangnail on his thumb.

Adrian started to pass a lot of people on their way to lunch at the campus cafeteria. Pretty soon he wasn't alone anymore. He was one of a crowd. Here they went, he and all the rest, to some important place in a hell of a rush. When he got near the Catholic Church next to the cafeteria he pulled ahead of most of the people.

This way, everybody. Keep calm and stick close to me. I'll get you through.

As he passed a nun, her cape bellied out and touched his hand. He looked back but her face was hidden by the cowl.

He would start like this: he would say, "Look, Katie," or "Here's the word, Katie," or he wouldn't say anything much.

"What's wrong?" she'd want to know. "Come on. What is it?"

"Nothing. Not really anything. But—."

He glanced back. The nun was going into the church and most of the other people had disappeared. The church's stained glass windows were sunlit. How much for one of those babies? A pretty penny.

Adrian turned up past the "enlist now" sign, the one with a marine holding a rifle in both hands. Some joker had torn hell out of the sign. Some pacifistic fanatic. Those pacifists didn't fool old sharp-as-a-razor Adrian, though. Not at all. It wasn't war they were against. It was risking their own bacon. They were looking out for number one just like everybody else. Just like Adrian himself. He was just more honest because he admitted it.

The Taylor Hall chimes started to chink out twelve. He was going to be late, damnit, and Katie might be guessing something was up.

If it would make her feel better, he might own that certain scenes would stick with him until he died. For instance the afternoon when they were kids and waded in Dickerson's creek. There stood Katie, ankle-deep, sobersides and skinny in those damned white cotton bloomers, picking up the crawdad he'd climbed the bank to get away from. There was a gem. Or maybe that would just make her madder.

When Adrian opened the glass door to the campus post office, he spotted Marion Drumm sitting on his fat ass behind the stamp window. Moonface Marion, the barber's son. Ate like a pig and looked like one. And, by god, he was growing a beard. A little bristly fringe. He thought he was one of the wild ones. One of the unwashed show-off fanatic bastards.

"How the hell are you, Moonface?"

"Hi. Well, HI! Say, this is great. I've seen you a couple of times across campus and waved like a nut but you didn't spot me."

"Gimme ten eight-centers, Moonface."

"That's eighty cents. Here's a weirdy to ponder. Just about everybody you see around this little old campus is from Kirby Falls. I mean don't it amaze you how many kids from Kirby Falls're registered here this term?"

"Yeah. It amazes the hell out of me."

"Eighty from a dollar. Except, of course, old horse-face Marilyn Dickerson. Her ma made her go to Cornell where SHE went. Out of state. Them rich Dickersons. What're you studying?"

"Ag-Ed."

"Boy, do I envy you, studying to be a teacher. I mean you got the brains to learn something that'll bring in some cabbage and get you some respect. My ma always comments on how wonderful you done in spite of your pa losing his pile and just eternally sitting around the house reading – uh – ."

"Thoreau."

"Me, I ain't got it up here nor in the pocketbook neither. I'm dropping out end of the term. Pa keeps putting the bee on me to come back and cut hair with him. He's getting, you know, old and he boozes it up. So I got to go back. How about having a bite of lunch with – ."

"I gotta date."

"Katie?"

"I'm supposed to be meeting her right now."

"Boy, it must be weird to have a girl you've known that long. I mean you must have dated her in diapers, for Crissake! Why, we all used to play Kick the Can and One a Cat together when Kate was an oddball kid."

"She's still an oddball kid."

"What's she studying?"

"Oh, art. Painting and stuff and English Lit. She putters. She just putters like hell. She'll never graduate. Like the rest of the clowns from Kirby Falls."

"Ain't it the truth? We all wind up back in Kirby Falls working for the Dickersons, ain't it awful. When you consider that they own my pop's shop and your ma's restaurant and Katie's old man's newspaper as, my god, what don't they? I suppose you'll teach at Kirby Falls High and you know who is president of the school board and tells the teachers when to wipe their noses."

"Christ Almighty!" Adrian exploded in spite of his colossal self-control. "Here's a little old bee for your bonnet, Moonface. Don't mention it around but I'm switching out of this goddamn collegiate extension of Kirby Falls. Yours truly got accepted two weeks back by Cornell to enter Veterinary Medicine there next term."

Adrian's teeth came together hard on the side of his tongue. 'Blabber-mouth,' he said to himself. 'Blabbermouth.' He looked at his watch. He could see the letter in the box. He thought he could see it. There was something pink.

"Vet Med!"

"Vet Med."

Because he said it so loud, two long-haired freaks turned around from the writing desk and stared at him.

Moonface shook his head. "That veterinary crap takes real dough," he said. "I hope you can scrape up the wherewithall."

"Gimme my change, Moonface."

"Ten-twenny. Say hello to Kate for me."

Adrian opened his box, took out three letters, slammed the box shut and kept going out the back door of the post office. One letter was pink as baby toes and had a lump in it. He pressed all over the envelope with thumb and forefinger. A very definite lump.

On the back steps of the post office he worked a small hole in the corner of the envelope, blew into it and squinted into the hole.

Click. Clickety-click. The old plan was going along like a main spring unwinding. Clickety-click.

But keep this in mind: try not to touch Kate's hands. Because if he did he'd mess up the bit. Because it was so sad how her hands were always sticky like a little kid's hands from the damndest things: oil, paint, turpentine, dutch chocolate, resin and even, one time, dandelion milk.

That was when they hid from the other kids on the Dickerson plot in the cemetery, behind those marble markers higher than their heads. And all the time Kate was calmly making this crazy chain out of dandelion stems. She put it on her sister's mound. Jenny that died of the scarlet fever. Her grave wasn't marked but Katie knew where it was. He was scared silly, walking on the graves, and when he grabbed her hand to run back it was sticky with dandelion milk.

So he'd keep clear of her and say, "Katie, this is how it is." Simple. It couldn't take more than half an hour. A scant twenty minutes. The worst she could do was throw a public fit.

Somebody was playing a tune on the chimes. "Stand up For Jesus," loud and martial as hell. Two maple leaves hit him in the face. He crossed the street and started down the steps. The wind up off the lake made the dropped leaves go jumping up and down like they were genuflecting. He lifted his heels higher from the ground at each step, putting his weight on his toes.

"At long, long last! Where on God's round earth have you been?

It's almost twelve-thirty. What are you, in a parade?"

Adrian dropped his books on the ground beside Katie. She had on a green blouse that looked about a hundred years old and denim pants. Her protest pants. Her passive resistance pants. She looked awful. Like something your mother gives to the Salvation Army.

She grabbed hold of his sleeve and pulled him down until he was sitting beside her. She perched on the bank so tucked in and little she hardly took up any room at all.

The sun in the lake was a yellow that hurt his eyes. On top of the sun, leaves were falling and floating. Katie had torn her paper bag open and spread her lunch out on it. Adrian took a package of cookies out of his back pocket and unwrapped it.

"Is that all you brought?"

"Yeah."

"I mean, is that one lousy pack of cookies ALL you brought?"

"Yes, it is."

"Take one of my sandwiches. Go ahead. This one's egg salad so take the peanut butter. Honest, Adrian—."

"I'm not hungry."

"Hungry your foot! You'd just die if anyone saw you bring your lunch in a bag."

"You look different."

"I quit curling my hair."

"Shouldn't you pin it back or something. I mean, can you see?"

"I'm going to let it grow down to my ankles."

"It looks terrible, Katie."

"But it's the real me. I mean it isn't phony any more. The curls were phony. Besides if I had a beard I'd look like Jesus."

"God!"

"You'll like it when it gets a little longer."

"You do the dumbest things. Do you realize that? Like that tattoo."

He pointed at the small red arrow on the back of her right hand.

"Everyone secretly wants to be tattooed," she said, eating her sandwich. "I was just brave enough to do it. You chickened out that night, if you remember."

"Your mother had a hemorrhage."

"She forgot they cut the cord. It's my skin now."

"Well, but a tattoo's phony as curls, isn't it?"

"No. It's a symbol."

"Of what?"

"Of us. You're the pure, seeking tip and I'm the feather to help you sail and give you balance. The shaft is love."

The wind blew the waxpaper from the peanut butter sandwich and wrapped it around Adrian's chin. The bite he had in his mouth stuck in his throat when he swallowed. He laid the sandwich down.

Katie grinned suddenly. "Don't look so glum," she said. "Nothing lasts forever. When we go to Europe the summer after you graduate, I'll probably shave my head and become a Bodhisattva."

Adrian rolled to his feet, pulling at the hangnail on his thumb.

Katie said, "What I want to see is the Sistine Chapel. I want to lie on my back on the floor of the Sistine Chapel and just stare up. For weeks. Then I'll come home and paint pictures inside the Kirby Falls ME Church."

Adrian snorted, his back toward her.

"What we'll do is, we'll go to Africa by way of the Sistine Chapel. It's the only way to go to Africa."

"Africa?"

"Yes. If we're going to join the Peace Corps I think we should go where we can do the most good. With your agriculture you should make the scene in Africa."

"What about you?"

"The little I've got to give, I can give anywhere. All I know how to do is scrub out latrines."

"You paint a little."

"A very little. Look at this."

Adrian turned around. She had pulled a canvas out of her portfolio and thrown it on the grass between them. He stared.

"When did you do that?"

"Last week."

"Why the hell did you do it? You won't ever paint anybody. Why did you want to do him? Like that? He looks like a goddamned Christian martyr or something."

"He was reciting Thoreau."

"God."

Adrian helped her pick up all the sandwich paper and walked

down by the lake with her while she threw it in the can.

"You could get twenty-five or fifty bucks out of Aunt Gert any time you'd paint her."

"It isn't finished. Your mother made him fiix a faucet or something so I couldn't finish it."

"Of all the family to pick out. I mean, honest to Jesus, Katie, don't you want to make something of yourself? Don't you want to be somebody?"

"I'm already somebody. I'm Kate."

"I mean, a commercial artist or something. For instance, why aren't you graduating when I am?"

"I've got some credits missing. I lost a term when I went with that bus load of kids down south to march with the blacks. I didn't take any science and I flunked expository speaking. I knew I would."

"Why'd you take it then?"

"I admire the idea of expository speaking."

"Well, that's what I mean. I mean you should want to be somebody. I sure as hell do. And we ought to be alike. Everybody in Kirby Falls laughs up their rears at your daddy's poker and Moonface Drumm's daddy's boozing and my daddy's Thoreau. Three goddamn clowns. Three bums. But not me. In a few years please just watch my dust."

"I've seen some already. Your mom's telling it all over Kirby Falls that you made the honorary, Phi Lambda Chi. You didn't even come close to making Phi Lambda Chi."

Adrian turned his back on the trash can and started walking around the lake at a pretty fast pace with Katie about a step and a half behind.

"When you were six you told her you saw elephants walking down Grove Street. In high school you told her you skipped a grade and she called the school and it wasn't so."

Adrian heard himself breathing like a cross-country runner. He slowed down and tried to look up to the top branches of the trees but the glinting sun in the water kept drawing his eyes back.

"The only trouble with you, Kate, is you're so stinking non sequitur. As a matter of fact all I ever meant to point out was, well, for example, I'll bet Marilyn Dickerson's old man would have paid you a hundred if you'd done her last summer when she wanted you to."

Katie had walked down along the brick wall close by the sulphur spring and was heaving little rocks at the lake. She skipped one seven times without even looking at it.

"Marilyn wouldn't have liked the finished product."

"How the hell can you—."

"I paint true and she wouldn't have liked it, that's all. Neither would her father. Neither would you."

The chimes had quit ringing and there was nothing but the wind blowing the leaves with a sound like dead bones rattling. He tore at his hangnail and a strip of skin jerked loose down nearly to the knuckle and it bled.

"Kate, I've been working around to mention—I'm entered into Veterinary Medicine at Cornell. I've been accepted and I'm going up Saturday to register."

She opened her hand and let the five stones that were in it fall beside her feet. She turned around and looked at him.

"I knew that."

"You knew that? How did you know it?"

"That's Kirby Falls for you. I just knew it."

"Well, goddamn it."

"Four more years. That's a long pull."

"And I'm not planning on using the old DVM in Africa either, Kate. Small animal medicine. Dogs and cats. That's where the money is. A clinic in New York or Chicago or Philly. In the suburbs where the well-heeled hang out. With a DVM after my name and an income in the upper bracket, I'll be somebody. That's what I want. I'm not ashamed of it.

"I know all that, too. By intuition."

"Well, why did you say all that about Africa, then?"

"I don't know. For the hell of it, I guess. Never mind, though. You can send the Africans a CARE package every Christmas."

"That's more than my old man's got the dough to do."

"I don't think our fathers are failures," Kate said in a quiet little voice that set his teeth on edge. "I think they're the only successes in Kirby Falls. Poker and Thoreau and booze got our fathers out of the rat race. All they live for now is enjoying themselves and being sweet to everyone. That's what everyone should live for, more or less."

"They live by kissing everybody's ass. Not me. Everybody'll be kissing mine."

"So that's all you want, is it?"

"Yes. It is. That's all anybody wants if they're honest. What do you want?"

"I don't know."

"Well, what? I'd really like to know."

He was standing close in front of her now with the round cement hole of the sulphur spring between them. The sulphur water was bubbling and it smelled terrible.

"I want cobalt blue."

"What?"

"Paint. A tube of blue paint. About the shade of a bluejay. And I want a sassafras tree to plant by my window at home."

"Kate—."

"But I don't want a new symbol. I can use the old one. That's what people ought to do with their old symbols: take a new look at them and keep using them. I'm frugal when it comes to symbols. That way you get layers of meaning like sedimentary rock."

She stretched out her hand and looked at it. It looked like a kid's hand, the fingers were so short and stubby. Anyone could see it was sticky.

"The arrow," she said, "stands for Navajo or Ute or Kiowa. It means I'll go clean latrines for the Indians."

Adrian scratched his head. "God, Kate. We aren't even talking about the same thing."

"Yes we are. We're both talking about Marilyn Dickerson."

"What?"

"Marilyn Dickerson. You've got her sorority pin. You think she's a pig but you're pinned to her and you're telling me gently to go to hell."

He took a step toward her but stopped at the rim of the spring.

"Katie—."

But she shook her head. "Because, God's truth that I just now realized it, it's this rare thing we had I've been trying so hard to say goodbye to all day and not you at all."

Adrian breathed in the sulphur smell. If he breathed in enough of it he might have a vision of the future like the oracle at Delphi. See if what was coming up was worth all this painful yakata-yak.

Kate stood with her head to one side looking into the sulphur spring. A leaf dropped into her hair. He stared at her funny small face and waited for her to say a word or two. Maybe she was thinking of something to say. He looked down too. He only saw the reflection of her face looking back up at him from the water.

Leaning over the spring that way their heads almost bumped. She reached out and took his hand. Then she let it drop like a stone. When he looked up she had got her portfolio and gone.

Adrian lifted one shoulder a quarter of an inch higher than the other and let it fall. He leaned down and dipped his hand in the spring, dipped it and dipped it until he began to notice the clowns passing by staring at him. Then he gathered up his books and went on about his business.

Ashur and Evir

All of the children who came to Miss Evir for piano lessons were frightened of her brother Ashur. His face made them tremble. He looked like a walking nightmare.

Scars drew down his eye and mouth corners and mottled his skin. Even his ears were nibbled about the edges.

Ashur, for his part, glowered at the children whenever they peeped into his study. The silly creatures distracted him from his accounts. He had no patience with them. He hated being disturbed at his figuring. It turned him physically ill.

On this particular morning, however, it was another diversion that pulled upon his attention.

From outside there came the clang of a cowbell and the slapping of boots. Ashur laid down his pencil and turned in his slow fretful manner until he faced the windows. The last of the dairy herd, thirty pure-bred Holsteins, sold the day before, were being led out of the barn and loaded into trucks by the new owners.

Ashur watched the cows come out of the milking parlour and down the path on the lead rope of the herdsmen. It was the last time they would walk the track their own feet had worn. Ashur was frightened to see them pass out of his possession. It heightened his sense of calamity and change. Life in its familiar aspect was dissolving away.

His mind recoiled so that he was scarcely able to reason at all. He watched the cattle with an uneasy gaze. He was seeing the end of his ownership here. However they had brought a good price.

The cows came stepping down the path one by one. They were fine animals, superb dairy types of thick girth with bony backs and jutting hooks. They swung their heavy heads up looking about with a vacant dignity, complacent in the intuition of their worth.

Two animals edged their ponderous bodies about until they faced back toward the barn and stretching out their pendulous necks, bawled uneasily. There they stood pawing in the mud of the path with their smooth well-trimmed hooves until the herdsman held out a scoop of grain. Then the cows moved forward once more daintily smelling of the feed, licking at it with their tongues.

At the loading ramps, now this cow now that one stood a moment, cold and mistrustful, was prodded from behind and so stepped up among the straws in the truck bed. The herdsmen secured the leadropes to the truck slats and fitted in the stock gate behind. Still the cows turned their heavy heads back toward the barn lowing fretfully. Every movement showed a longing for the familiar security of the stanchion left behind, bewildered recoil from the dangers of the shifting, flimsy truck.

When all the cattle were loaded, the herdsmen climbed behind the steering wheels, ignited the engines, and pulled away turning out onto the highway in single file. The cattle stood swaying, shifting their weight, almost stumbling. They raised their heads to look back but in the end rode away content enough in the apprehension of their own significance.

Ashur watched the cattle until the last stock truck moved off down the hill and only a trace of dust remained above the road. The dairy herd was almost the fingers of his hands to him. He felt weakened, aimless, vulnerable before the world now.

The morning mail had brought an expected letter confirming the sale of the farm. Life as Ashur had known it was finished. He sat with his sister in the study attempting to approach the reality of his new situation. The curtains were down. The room already looked forlorn. The heavy dark wall cupboards themselves seemed waiting to be abandoned.

Ashur pushed away from the desk, stood up and opened the

door out onto the porch. He clucked to the few White Rock hens scratching in the yard and threw them a handful of corn out of his jacket pocket.

He spat into the dust by the stoop and waited, observing the hens as they ran up in a flurry to peck up the grains. Afterward they wandered about dolefully cocking their eyes up at him, hoping for more. He viewed them absently until they began to scratch again in the dirt of the yard, still looking up at him now and again and uttering querulous questioning squawks. Then he nodded his head saying to them,

"You'll be getting little more corn of me, won't you, biddies? I'll not gather your eggs many more nights."

The hens shook their wattles stupidly, wandered away by ones and twos and fell to pecking at the grapevines on the fence. They too would soon pass out of his dominion.

A musing stillness settled on the room. Ashur returned to sit before his account books. He was loath to leave the room before he understood his sister's intentions.

Taking up the pencil he made several figures, then looked over at Evir who sat, taking no notice of him, sorting over her sheets of music. An extremely lively woman of seventy, she cared nothing for the farm affairs. Her movements were quick and exuberant, even rather joyful. 'Harum-scarum' her brother called her.

"You'd best turn your share of the money over to the Home as I plan to do," he advised her.

He was well satisfied with the place. He had inspected a great number of retirement establishments and settled on the Home as offering him the best deal for his money, the most iron-clad security. He would be cared for, kept at his ease, until his death. He would have liked a word or two of praise for his shrewdness.

However, his sister, examining her music with eager attention, did not comment.

"You'll come along, won't you? There's little else you can do."

The woman did not raise her head.

"You couldn't rent a room in town much less buy your food on what you're paid for teaching piano," Ashur went on querulously. "Your pupils have already fallen off. You'll soon turn senile and not able to teach. It behooves you to face facts. If you go on your own, your part of the money from the farm will soon be used up. I can tell you that. And you'll have doctor bills and clothes to pay for besides."

Evir took no notice of him.

"But what did you think to do, fussing with that music all the morning?" he said looking at her rather coldly.

"I'm giving a recital at the church this evening. Had you forgotten?" she said gently.

As it happened, he had forgotten.

"Now that's a waste of time. A recital's properly given as advertisement to attract students. You won't be teaching any more."

"Won't I?"

"You know you won't. You do plan to go to the Home, don't you? The matter should be settled at once."

But she went on with the music and did not answer.

"You ought to decide, Evir. Your name must be entered at once if you're to be let in. The money must be paid."

"Must it?" she said absently.

"You've no idea of money."

"No."

"You'll end at the Poor Farm starving amongst the penniless and the looneys."

"Yes," she said.

But he could see she paid little mind to him. He had talked through her and around her since their childhood. She was born impractical. Let her go her way, then. He must look out for himself.

The scrape of bicycle tires came on the porch, then a rap at the doorframe.

"Step in," Ashur called out impatiently.

The boy, Sam Elliott, an orphaned ward of the county, came softly into the room holding his cap and a ragged music book.

"Well, Sam."

"Mr. Ashur, the cows is gone," the boy burst out with a look of death itself.

"Yes. Whipple trucked the last of them off this morning."

"And you'll be going soon, too?"

"Yes."

"But I thought it would be longer before you left."

"No. And your job's going with us. I won't need you to help any more, Sam. Sit down if you've a mind to."

The boy sank onto the edge of a chair. His eyes followed Evir as she busied herself opening various charts and music books with her quick nervous hands. She wound the metronome.

"I wish you wasn't going," the boy murmured.

He was a bony youngster with a small soft underjaw not yet developed into a man's look. His front teeth were irregular and too large for his mouth. He wanted a hair cut: fair bristles bushed out over his ears. His eyes were blue, wide and easily affected. His shoulders bent forward hollowing his narrow chest. There was about him a lost, tentative manner, a frightened air that reminded Ashur of himself as a boy, after the fire; of the boy he had been.

"You liked working here, did you?" Ashur said looking at Sam with his cold, rather vacuous expression.

"I did, yes."

"Liked the dairy. Likely you'd've bought my cows. I should have offered you the chance."

Ashur nodded his heavy white head humorously.

"And I suppose you won't be here to plant the wheat next month?" said the boy disappointedly.

"No. I'll be off and away," Ashur said. "You were good enough help, Sam. Some other farmer'll put you to use."

The boy turned slowly in his chair and watched Evir switch on the lamp and roll back the cover off the keys with her lively preoccupied manner.

"Is Miss Evir going to the Home along with you?"

"She won't say what she means to do," Ashur observed fretfully. "I told her to come, but she'll never listen to what I say. The whole county respects my opinion on financial matters but not so my own sister."

"Why, what will happen to her then?"

"God knows," said Ashur angrily. "God knows. If she's here yet next week, she'll be put out in the road."

"This is my last lesson," Sam said wonderingly.

"Carry over your stool, Sam," Evir said. "I'll hear your recital piece first all through slowly. And then the scale."

Ashur watched Sam sitting beside the old woman playing his

lesson. His sister had also taught him to play as a boy. She was five years older than he. He was surprised how clearly he recalled her small quick freckled hands touching his, setting his fingers right and how she had spoken to him rapidly of the music in her bright intense way, wanting him to know about the pieces. It came to him that she had talked to him about himself, also, as they sat at the piano: about his own secrets which mattered excessively to him.

After the lesson, Ashur walked with the boy out of the house and slowly across the yard to the barn where Sam's bicycle leant in the doorway.

The house they left had a forlorn look. It had been a handsome sturdy building once, but now the foundation under the north side was sunken and the spouting rusted, although the section rebuilt after the fire had a stouter look. The newly abandoned barn appeared warped and in need of paint. The house and the farm buildings were beginning to show their considerable years. With the heart of the farming operation, the cattle, trucked away, the place had an air of sterile ruin, bewilderment, and decay.

Now that his own age and that of the farm equipment and buildings threatened Ashur's efficiency, he was shrewd enough to barter the farm for the firmer security of the Home.

"It was a good herd," Ashur said looking about the barn, hardly aware that he spoke aloud. "We shipped Grade A and a lot of it. The milk check made a nice sum every month.

"And we took firsts on the show circuit every fair time. A whole string of blue ribbons last year. Beat out a lot of other men's cattle.

"The ribbons weren't for sport," Asher continued querulously but feeling proud. "They brought the cattle buyers in to look for breeding stock. That's advertising. Dairy farming run right is damn big business."

He shook his head, rubbing the scarred flesh of his cheeks, thinking seriously about what he said. "You can lose a sackful of money or make one. Depends on how sharp you are. I watched out for myself. I knew no one else would watch out for me.

"After the fire, this farm lost money for years. I was the one made it pay its debts, put it over into the black. I built my operation around the cattle. I worked dawn until dark to bring them into full production. Dawn until dark. Never an idle day."

When the boy's bicycle tires flung back gravel as he rode off, Asher was startled. He had forgotten the child was with him.

Ashur had never attended one of his sister's recitals. He pooh-poohed her music as a waste of time. When she gathered her little ones together he had business in the barns.

Tonight, however, the barns were empty.

Ashur sat scowling in the study, winding up his records while the house began to fill with the sound of children's voices. He heard quick footsteps scraping about the rooms he and Evir usually kept shut off. After their parents died in the fire, brother and sister had lived economically in only a part of the lower floor.

Now the unaccustomed activity carried him back to the farm as it had been under his parents' sway; a cheerful busy homeplace used to the bustle and shouts of work going forward. After the fire a change had come over the rooms. An unspoken fear had taken possession of the house.

Ashur left his desk and prowled restlessly about the study. It troubled him that Evir would not declare her plans. He realized that little talk had passed between them through the years. Still, if he was absorbed in his dairy, he certainly had been conscious of her doing for him all this time; tidying the house, washing up his overalls and socks, cooking the food in her energetic fashion. He felt obliged to her, certainly. She had raised him after all, and he knew what he owed her. She had saved his life, if it must be repeated. Everyone knew she had caught him as he ran, afire and screaming, out the door and rolled him over and over in the wet snow. He would never deny it. He didn't propose to move off and leave her to fall destitute and homeless. For it could come to that, as she had no business sense.

In the kitchen he found Evir shoveling hot cookies out of the oven. Her face was suffused with a warm flush. Heat from the stove, he supposed, and yet how lively it made her appear; how thoroughly alive as if it came, rather, from within herself. The whole atmosphere of the house, the stirring in every part of it, startled Ashur. The smell of the cookies reminded him of how his mother had used to bake sometimes in the evening.

"Now, Ashur, you must certainly stand out of my way or you will be thrown down and stamped upon," Evir cried humorously and she poked a broken piece of cookie into his mouth, taking him by surprise.

When it came time to drive to the church, Ashur with a grimace put himself into a clean shirt. He might as well go, he thought. It would be the last recital, after all.

Evir and a hoard of the country children climbed into the farm truck. Ashur handed in the cookies. He discharged his passengers at the church door and himself parked the truck down the street and walked back.

The town was still. The evening air, moist and close, smelt of autumn decay. Ashur turned up his collar and walked hesitantly through the long shadows of the houses. His strange nibbled ears gave him an odd look in the intermittent light.

The brick sidewalk where he stepped pushed down upon the roots of the trees that lined the street, constraining their growth. Dead leaves lay thick and wet in the gutters. The silver water tower swelled above the duller smaller bell tower of the church.

Ashur looked back up the street to where his farm truck was pulled up beside the curb. He could see the worn use-blackened stock gate, the straw sticking up from the truck bed, the high muddy tires.

Well, he would never load cattle into that truck again, nor ride to the fair bouncing on the springs of the high front seat. The cattle were sold. The farm was passing into other hands. The only place he cared to be in the whole county was gone; the work that had absorbed him was over. Still he would be secure in his old age.

Ashur viewed the lighted church windows with misgivings. He loitered on the steps. A group of people passed in before him, flinging the door wide. Ashur had a glimpse of the shadowed sanctuary and the piano rolled out before the communion rail; above, the organ pipes, below, the carpeting. He caught sight of his sister facing the filled pews. He stepped suddenly in at the door.

As he moved down the aisle, he was apprehensive of passing under the shadows of the rafters. The dread touched him briefly like the mood of a dream. The people in the pews turned their heads to watch after him. He sat down self-consciously in the back of the church and fell to kneading his hat between his fingers. All the while he kept an eye upon Evir, for it seemed to him that the heavy shadows reaching down from the ceiling would soon cover her over.

The people of the audience, even the boy now performing at the piano, were obscured by the gloom.

After the piece was played, Evir ran forward in her lively way and, catching hold of the small boy, gave him such a squeeze that he gasped and giggled. She turned to the audience, still holding the squirming performer, and cried out,

"This child is a special one. He can accomplish such astounding things when he puts his mind to it! I think he's an exceptional person. You watch. You'll all be amazed at what he'll do."

After each child performed, she did and said the same. No one doubted that it was true of each one.

Ashur leant forward, musing, for she had used to say that of him. All down the years she had said it. She said it still, now and again.

A bar of shadow fell across his shoulder and he drew back, startled. Being in the church recalled to his mind how he had used to come with his family as a boy. They had come in a line, walking down the aisle: first his father, then his mother, then Evir, and he last of all. So they had come, all in a line, holding hands.

His hired boy sat down to the piano. When the boy spread out his music, Ashur saw that his hands were shaking. He made a false start, began again, stopped, played on a while, hit a discord and stopped again. He hid his face on the music rack.

"There," said Evir. "What does it matter? Begin again."

She sat down on the bench beside him while he played the piece through.

But at the end he wept again and, turning toward her with a streaming face, sobbed out,

"Don't go away! Don't. Don't!"

"There," she said quickly. "There, now."

"Whatever'll I do if you go away?" he said.

But she laughed and rocked him back and forth on the piano bench with her small freckled hands until he stopped his complaining.

"Now you are all to have cookies downstairs," she said. "And Sam will pour out the punch. I'll let no one except Sam touch the pitcher, you understand, because he does it so well."

They trooped off, all of the people, little and big, except Evir who busied herself closing the piano and gathering up her music, and her brother Ashur who still sat in a back pew of the sanctuary in his clean shirt.

"Well, Ashur," she said, pausing at the sight of him there.

"I was sitting here recalling," he mused, "how often you said 'there' to me when I was a boy, after the fire."

"Eh, we had need to say 'there' to one another often enough in those days. We were afraid then."

"I was but surely you never were, Evir."

"Why, yes. I was afraid, too. Of course I was."

"And are you at all afraid now, Evir?" he asked curiously.

"Now I haven't time," she told him, laughing. "I haven't the time to spare. Ha ha! That's the truth."

The others began to come up from the basement and say good-night. Ashur watched them lean down, stretch out their hands to Evir, smile and move out into the darkness.

Last of all Sam came and stood by Evir saying earnestly and shyly, "One day I'll buy a house, Miss Evir."

"Yes," the old woman said gently.

"I've saved from my wages and from my paper route."

"Then you'll have it," she said. "I think you will if you want it."

"You can come there. You can live with me."

"Thank you. I'll come, then."

"But are you going away?" he pressed her. "I won't want to do it if you go away."

"I think, after all, I'll not go away," she told him, considering. "I believe that I might rent a room in town and move in my piano and stay a while."

"I'd be glad," he said.

Brother and sister were alone in the truck driving home. Ashur spoke out, wishing to see the matter settled.

"Then you've decided you won't come to the Home with me?" he asked.

"I've decided I won't come."

"If you fall into hard times, I can't help you."

"That's as it must be. Don't think about it."

Exasperated, he let the matter drop. He considered he had argued enough. If she would not go on sensibly, he must at least watch out for himself.

He pressed the gas peddle down. He wished to get home quickly and go to bed though he knew he would not sleep. He was always wakeful at night and lay long turning on his mattress. When he slept at last he was often troubled by evil dreams. He supposed he would sleep as badly in the Home since sleeplessness was in his nature.

The Great Tomato War

She watched uneasily but with a measure of admiration as her elder sister Selma bit into a large ripe tomato. The juice gushed down her chin.

"You don't know what's good!" Selma cried.

Dolly nervously rubbed the tomato in her own hand along her sleeve to clean it and brought it to her lips.

"Go on, scaredy cat," shouted Selma. She looked like a queen standing spraddle-legged and fearless in the sunny garden with tomato juice running down to her elbows.

"It'll drip all over me."

"Let it drip, that's all. Go on and bite in, you goose."

Dolly bit unhappily. There was a pop as the skin parted easily under her teeth and the turgid juice filled her mouth and splashed her face. She almost gagged.

"Yuk!" Dolly said.

"What?"

"It's the taste. I don't like the old tomatoey taste."

"That's the best taste on earth," Selma chanted marching up and down as if she were leading an army.

Dolly saw that her sister's shorts and blouse were stained with tomato juice. They were too small for Sel anyway, who, at twelve, was growing like rising bread. Dolly hoped the tomato would wash out because she would be wearing those clothes in a month's time.

"I say we bury our Solemn Oath right here, by the tomato vines," Selma crowed.

She had got a spade and she stuck it into the earth portentiously.

"But our Solemn Oath is tin, Sel. It'll get all rusty and spoiled if we put it in the ground. Besides, once the ground freezes we can't get at it. Let's put it in my bottom dresser drawer."

"Somebody'll see it there, ninny."

"Nobody will. Nobody ever pokes in my drawer. I keep all my private items there."

But Selma shook her head with its stiff blond hair that stuck up like a rooster's comb and began to dig. Dolly lifted the plaque holding it reverently by the extreme edges.

She and Sel had flattened out a tin can and written on it a terrible oath with their blood ending: 'We will be true forever to our solemn oath of loyalty.'

Selma had contrived the wording. Dolly wasn't clear what it meant. However, she stood in awe of it.

"We'll bury it here deep down as we can dig," Selma panted, her nostrils flared wide. "And we'll never touch it on pain of death, until we grow up and move away. Then we'll dig it up at midnight and cut it in two with the tin shears and each carry half to our dying day."

"But suppose we change our minds about what it says before then," Dolly fretted. "Can't we dig it up sooner?"

"No sir, we can't or it'll bring a curse down on our heads. This afternoon we'll build our club house in the corner of the garden facing this spot."

It was late summer and the tomato vines wilted in the heat. Dolly found the garden with its odor of over-ripe and rotting vegetation unbearably musky and fetid. The garden was quiet but from Sullivant Avenue a block away the sounds of buses and automobiles rumbled night and day. They had moved to the city from farming country where there was no traffic. The noise of the cars pulled at Dolly's consciousness, tingling and provocative like the sense of autumn coming. The two together, autumn and the traffic, made Dolly uneasy. A turn-over was on the way.

"I can't build the club house this afternoon," she said to Selma plucking up her courage at last.

"What?"

"Don't get mad. I can't help it. I promised Mrs. Dillon across the alley I'd mind her children."

"Why did you do that?" Selma shouted. "You knew we were going to build today."

"She asked me."

"Well, why didn't you say 'no,' you goose? We've only got today. School starts tomorrow. It'll take us hours and hours."

"Mrs. Dillon burned her arm and she has to go to the doctor."

Selma stood still, her stocky legs planted one on either side of the hole she had dug. She scowled.

"Listen to those cars," she brought out suddenly, grimacing with her teeth shut so that she looked like a threatening dog. "I hate those cars. They go all day and all night. I hear them every second. It was quiet on the farm. As soon as we're grown, we'll buy back the farm, Doll. We'll go live there. You and me."

Dolly watched her sister lay the tin plaque in the hole and cover it over with earth. She felt weighted down as if she herself were going into the ground.

"I hate Mrs. Dillon," Selma said. "You're not to go."

"I promised."

"It doesn't matter. What has dumb old Mrs. Dillon got to do with us? You have to help me build the club house. If you don't, you'll break your sacred oath that we just made and buried. You know you will. Then you'll be sorry!"

"Why will I?"

"I'll make you sorry. You know I can."

Dolly was a small person, spare and shy and always rather apprehensive. Her hair was long and dark. It lay heavy on her shoulders dragging her down. She had thought to cut it short in the spring but Selma admired it. Dolly held it up now, catching it into a bunch and baring her neck to what breeze there was.

"I'm going to Mrs. Dillon's," she said firmly, astounding herself.

"You're not," said Selma. She screamed it. "You're not! You're not! You're not!"

"How can we be a club anyhow, Sel," Dolly said, musing, "just the two of us?"

"Because together we are safe. Alone we're just me and you. You better watch out."

"I'm going," said Dolly and she actually walked away through the tomato vines.

Even she herself did not believe she would go. She moved along waiting to see what Selma would do. When Dolly reached the lawn where the grasses were beginning to wither and curl, a sudden gush of cold water caught her underneath, climbing her legs icily, spurting up as high as her arm pits, wetting her clothes, her face, her hair.

"You turn off that sprinkler!" she gasped. "You turn it off. You turn it off."

She retreated back into the garden away from the malicious, spouting water.

"You've got to stay, Doll," Selma said. "On account of the oath we swore."

"All right. I'll help you a while. But then I'll go to Mrs. Dillon."

After she had carried boards for a long time, Dolly looked at her smarting hands. She had got blisters on both of her palms. Her clothes were already dried in the heat and sweated wet again. As she passed the fresh earth where the plaque was buried, she felt a dark outrageous pull upon her. All her life she had been aware of a coercion. Never had she known its exact location before. Now, there it lay, buried in that hole.

Dolly worked faithfully on the club house until the middle of the afternoon. Selma was good at carpentry. She made a strong frame and they began to nail on the boards to form the walls.

"Now, I'm going," Dolly said when she thought she must. She laid down her hammer.

"But it isn't half begun yet," Selma wailed. "I can't finish it myself."

"I promised Mrs. Dillon."

"All right. Go. But you'll be sorry. You'll see."

When Dolly returned toward evening, she observed that the club house was not much farther along. She could hear Selma hammering inside the half-raised walls.

She went indoors to put away her wages. In her room she found her bottom dresser drawer dumped out on the floor.

All her private most secret possessions lay helter-skelter on the rug. She stared at them bewildered. Then, kneeling, she began to pick them up gingerly, cautiously, as if they were bleeding.

When she finished and went outside, it was coming dusk. Selma was still hammering inside the club house. Dolly walked to where the spade lay beside the tomato vines. She picked it up and used it to uncover the plaque. By beating on the tin sheet with the shovel she pitted it into illegibility and crumpled it into a ball which she tossed far down the alley. She stuck the shovel upright in the soft earth of the resurrection site.

Then she picked up a tomato and threw it with a smack against the half-raised wall of the club house. It burst upon the boards and oozed downward in an obscene red smear.

Selma came out of the club house and stared.

With awful concentration Dolly went on throwing tomatoes.

"You stop that!" Selma screamed. "Are you crazy? You stop."

And she herself picked up a tomato and let fly directly at Dolly. After that they threw to hit one another. A steady stream of soft overripe tomatoes flowed between the two girls, a dark bitter unremitting barrage.

They threw hard and accurately and with a perfect frenzy. When they were hit, they grunted and reached for another tomato. Their clothes, their faces, their hair became plastered with red pulpy residue and still they threw.

Nothing had ever delighted Dolly so much as the feel of the warm tomatoes under her fingers. How beautifully her arm and shoulder muscles bunched and sent the fruit soaring. She listened with satisfaction and exhilaration to the mushy splat. Another hit. Think of that: another hit! She laughed aloud and threw again and so on into the blackening night.

Selma was the first to quit the field of battle. She ran away dripping across the lawn.

Dolly, left alone, spattered and breathless, stood listening to the distant traffic on Sullivant Avenue. She thought it a rather pleasant noise. It carried the pulse of life going forward.

Coon Hunt

Nobody saw Quenby get out. Clara Fortune went to feed her and she was gone from the house, that was all.

"Quenby. You, Quenby!"

But you can't call a cat like you do a dog, can you?

"Kitty, kitty, kitty."

Pedigreed and not allowed to roam. Came into the house at six weeks old and never set foot out of it until now, seven years later. Why would she want to and her cushion so cozy and her food set out?

"Look under the porch," Mama had said, "and in the bushes."

Mama's voice was always warm and coaxing like a brood hen's.

Not in the bushes. Not in the long grass around the cistern top. The last light burst through cloud low in the west, brightening the saltbox shape of the Fortune house.

A star showed through the top branch of the oak like a tear in an eyelid and the sunset wind moaned amongst its shaggy leaves. Booth's woods lay below, dark as deep water.

Clara threw herself on her back beside the porch steps. The day lilies around her were closed to shapes like fingers. The rising moon was white. There were moths on the screen.

Behind her breastbone all this summer there'd been flutterings like wings. She thought her soul was trying to come out but Mama said it was only her blood pounding because she ran too hard.

"Quenby?"

She crawled through the hole in the lattice and under the house, a tight squeeze. Only a year ago she'd darted in and out like a fish. Now her shoulders and breasts caught though the rest of her was skinny enough still. A beanpole, a stile, a step ladder of a girl. Over her head she could hear Mama's quick light steps.

Clara found, not Quenby, but a nest with five eggs still warm from the hen. She put the eggs inside her blouse and slid out on her back. Coming around the house corner, she saw the end of the oak branch over the porch roof whip and set the leaves a-quiver. She put the eggs in the porch box.

Up it for sure and can't get down.

Clara swung herself onto the lowest limb. She climbed, scraping her knees and elbows, until she was on a level with the second floor window. There sat Papa on his and Mama's bed with his galluses turned down. Across the hall she could see, in her own room, the chair with the red cushion on which Quenby usually dozed, purring, every afternoon.

Clara climbed higher to where the tree, still full of sun, swung in the breeze like a tolling bell. From this high she could see the complete round of the yard, already in shadow. There were Mama's flowerbeds, bright from the coming cold, round and square, triangle and rectangle with wire fencing at the edges. There was the woodshed and her bicycle leaning against it and the pear tree where her old swing drifted to and fro.

A scratching on the bark.

"Quenby?"

Clara climbed higher until her fingers closed on a warm smoothness. No cat. What, then? Clara tilted her head, staring up. A face looked back at her through the leaves. She held the branches aside and found Floyd Kilkinney perched in a crotch like a possum.

He opened his fist and showed her three locust skins sitting on the palm. Looking close, Clara saw locust skins everywhere clutched to the bark, staring back at her with empty eye bubbles.

She climbed up to where Floyd sat. He smelled of the fields, of dew and sumac and sassafras. He had locust shells stuck to his clothes and in his hair.

He moved his leg until it touched hers all along the calf. His face was in shadow but she felt his breath quicken against her neck.

She said, "I thought you was Quenby."

"That Quenby's gone off with some tom," he said.

He leaned down of a sudden and pushed his mouth hard against hers so that her lips puffed and stung and a strong pulsing began in her throat.

He settled back triumphant.

"I told you I'd do that before this day was done," he said.

All at once he lifted his head.

"Hark!"

They held their breath. Far off across Booth's woods came a thin piping. When Floyd said, "That's Uncle Garret's Liza up front," she knew it was hounds after a coon.

"Doesn't your uncle ever get lost hunting in Booth's woods?" she asked him. "Papa won't let me go in it because he says I'd never find my way out."

"Uncle Garret gets lost. So do I. That's half the fun."

Floyd dropped a locust skin into her lap. "There's one never made it," he said.

The shell felt heavy as a bullet. Sure enough there was the dead locust, greenish and dull-eyed, still inside. She shivered and let it fall, hearing it hit branches as it dropped. The sun was suddenly gone from the tree as if a lamp had been blown out.

Floyd wound his leg around hers and kissed her again. The kiss lasted so long they both gasped at the end of it.

"Let's get the hell out of this before we fall out," Floyd said.

They inched down the trunk, hung by their hands from the lowest branch and dropped into a pool of shadow.

Floyd flopped belly-down in the grass.

"Let's run off and get married," he said.

Clara sat beside him, Indian-style. Till the day he came to help her papa make Fortune hay, she'd thought boys were silly. But his eyes, black and wild as sin, picked her out and picked her out wherever she stood. Soon he was talking to her every chance he got, she watching his soft, curving mouth shape the words.

All that summer he hung around her and on into autumn like a hummer at a blossom. Winter he came and waited in first light to walk her to school and waited by the school door to walk her home when last light was coming on.

The next spring he was still around her. Then the summer day she surprised him drinking at the Fortune well, he looked at her with water running down his chin and said, solemn as a sage, "This fall, we'uns'll get married."

She didn't say no. He was her choice, same as she was his. But when fall came, she didn't feel ready so she said, "In six months." And when that was up, she said, "In six months more."

And now that was up and she said, "We ain't got a dollar betwixt us, Floyd. We'd starve to death inside a week."

"I got the promise of a job at the sawmill down to Beloit on the river," he told her. "After we save some money, we'll go on down to New Orleans. I always wanted to look on the Gulf."

"I ain't going."

"Yo're scared to leave home, is all. Age you are, my ma'd been a wife two years. Yo're scared to let go of yore mama and papa. Chicken liver!"

Clara buried her fingers in Floyd's hair and gave a pull. It was so crisp and springy it started her fingertips tingling. Locust shells fell from it right and left. It was too lively to hold them.

He gripped her wrists one in each hand and bent her backward. They swayed, then toppled flat on the ground where he held her arms pinned wide, leaned his forehead against her neck and blew his breath down her blouse so that all of her skin prickled.

He was quick as a weasel and too strong for her. Sweat from his chin dropped into her eyes and her mouth. It had a tangy taste like ocean water.

Twisting sideways out of his grip, she grabbed up one of the eggs from the porchbox and pelted it against his chest. It broke, the yellow popping like a bubble and spattering him chin to knee.

"By god, you'll answer for that!" he said through his teeth.

Scooping up the other four eggs, he caught her in the back with one as she ran through the yard and on the shoulder with another as she went down the hill. At the edge of the woods, she stopped to look back and the third egg caught her on the thigh.

Still she'd outfox him. He'd never get her with the last one. She slipped in under the trees where it was dark as a cave. She walked until she stumbled over a rotten log by a run of water, then crouched behind it.

She didn't hear him coming but suddenly he swept back the bushes so the moon, gone yellow now, shone on her.

"You look good enough to fry for breakfast," he said. "Here, you can throw the last one so you won't hold me no grudge."

He held out the egg cupped on his palms ready to snatch it away when she reached for it. Quicker than thought she clapped his two hands together. He stood staring at his dripping fingers until she moved off, then, with one lunge, caught her by the skirt.

Pulling free, she gave him a push that sent him reeling backwards into the creek. He came out of the water shaking himself like a wet dog.

Floyd reached for her, bent on giving her a ducking, but she made off into the woods. He came after her, running. They ran until suddenly dogs were barking all around them and there stood Floyd's Uncle Garret with several other men beside a small campfire.

The flames lit a great tree around which dogs were leaping and yelping. One large yellow bitch was baying with a deep bell tone. Clara followed the raised noses of the dogs with her glance until she saw masked, bright eyes and a furry body on a high limb.

"Hold her, Liza!" the men whooped. "Hold her, girl."

They heaped dry leaves and light limbs on the fire and stood about it, staring up. Clara, too, couldn't take her eyes off the coon. When the fire brightened she saw black hands gripping the bark, heaving sides and the pricking of small pointed ears.

Floyd stepped into the firelight, kicking off his shoes. He shed his shirt like an old skin and stood for a moment gazing at the coon.

Then he was across the clearing and up the tree, pulling himself hand over hand up the grapevines that matted the trunk until he gripped the bare, curving lower limbs with his knees. The firelight shone on his dark skin as the muscles moved beneath it. The dogs leaped higher, yelping louder. The coon, immobile as a statue, watched Floyd climb toward her. Her lip was lifted from her teeth and her nose wrinkled in a snarl. As he drew nearer, her body quivered, her hands gripped tight to the bark and she crouched lower, gathering her feet under her. A rank, pungent odor coming from the coon filled the air.

As Floyd climbed higher, the coon backed away from the trunk, edging further out onto the limb.

"Keep a tight hold. Don't you slip," Uncle Garret shouted to Floyd. "Whatever falls from that tree, these here dogs is going to tear to pieces, boy or coon, don't matter which."

Clara looked at the hounds. Their long teeth were like knife blades and their tongues licked in and out.

Floyd reached the limb where the coon perched and began to shake it, bracing himself against the trunk and using both hands.

How tight the furry thing clung to her place! She must be dizzy from whipping up and down. Still she hung on. There on the branch, the coon looked like a cat. Like Quenby. But a wild Quenby. A Quenby gone mad.

"Fall, you goddamned varmint, fall!" the men shouted.

Floyd rested against the trunk, breathing hard. Through the leaves, Clara saw the coon's shiny eyes looking at the dogs.

Floyd shook the limb mightily. Clara's mouth gaped open. The coon sprang as though she would soar away, then fell on the dogs, limbs spread.

The hounds, in their scramble to get at the coon, scattered the fire so that the clearing fell into sudden darkness.

Clara could hear the snapping of the dogs' teeth, their yelps and their growling, the screeches of the coon and hoarse hollering of the hunters above the din.

Wild and sightless, the men ran this way and that, bumping into now one another, now the trees or bushes as they tried to keep from being bitten by the dogs or scratched and bitten by the coon.

The fight subsided. Silence fell on the woods. The men kicked the embers together and piled on dry leaves and branches until the fire blazed up once more.

The hounds, bleeding from torn ears and bitten muzzles, milled about whining while Floyd lifted up the dead coon, dripping blood and urine, from their midst and held her high above their heads. From her ripped and bloody face, the coon's half-closed eyes looked out with a dreamy stare.

Uncle Garret danced a jig and pounded Floyd on the back. All the men cheered and shouted and talked at once, relating the hunt to one another while they brought out fruit jars and passed them around. Floyd came up to Clara holding out a jar.

"Since you're a coon hunter now, you might as well finish up right with a drink of corn," he said.

He was laughing and panting, his shoulders heaving. Sweat glistened on his chest and in his hair.

Numb to the lips from the coon's drop, Clara took the jar in her hands and looked into it at the raw colorless liquid. All the men were smiling, watching her, the firelight flickering on their faces. She raised the jar and drank.

At once she began to gasp and to beat at her throat and her chest where she felt a thousand matches suddenly lit and flaming.

The men roared. Uncle Garret fell on the ground and rolled. Clara wheezed and sputtered. When at last her breath came easier, a glow began in her belly and spread to all her parts until her skin was a-blaze and her insides filled with heat and she thought she had fallen into the fire and herself become the flames, leaping, devouring the leaves and branches, giving off an astounding brightness.

Afterwards, she slipped to her knees and began to retch. She heaved and heaved again while Floyd held her forehead and the trees marched around and around them like soldiers. She ended, tired out and sobbing, and, weak as a day-old kitten, fell asleep against Floyd's chest.

When she woke, the fire had burned to a red ash and the men and dogs were gone. Floyd sat beside a lantern watching her.

"God a'mighty!" he burst out. "I thought you was poisoned and yore death coming on you."

Then he threw back his head and laughed until tears stood in his eyes.

"If yo're going to hunt coon, you got to learn to hold yore corn better than that," he said.

Clara stood up, mortified to the roots of her soul.

"I'm going home," she said and moved quickly off into the woods.

The blackness was full of briars and branches and night animals that started up under her feet with a great noise and ran off. She tripped over roots and walked into bushes. Behind her came Floyd swinging the lantern at his side, laughing to himself.

She began to walk faster, looking to come out on the road below the Fortune house. However, no way she turned seemed right. She went on and went on and still there was nothing but trees. In front, behind, to left, to right, only trees.

A few stars shone down through high branches. She stopped, started off to the right, then turned left. Floyd came behind her, laughing.

"Which way?" she asked him over her shoulder. "Why don't you tell me which way?"

She stopped so that he walked into her. Feeling his chest come against her, she pounded it with her fists until her face was hot and her breath came in gasps.

"Show me the right way to go," she said, almost crying. "Pretty soon you'll get lost yourself. Then we'll never get out. We'll die in Booth's woods."

He gripped her arms so she couldn't pound him and kissed her neck, then down onto her breasts. His mouth was everywhere, pressing against her from every direction, scattering her out into the dark.

She heard a screech owl cry close beside them, then again further off. The woods swelled full of murmurs and clicks, scrapes and calls, whistles and barks, rustles and sighs. Loudest of all were the tree frogs, buzzing like the locusts in the day only more shrill and not so loud.

Floyd laid his head on her shoulder and she felt his face hot through her sleeve. They stood without moving while the moon climbed over their heads and filtered down amongst the leaves.

When she tried to pull away, he held her fast.

"Clarie, meet me by the highway bridge tomorrow night," he whispered, muffled, into her hair. "We'll hitch to Kentucky and find a J.P. Come when the moon clears Booth's woods. Clarie, will you come?"

And wouldn't turn loose of her wrists until she'd nodded her head.

When Clara stepped out of the woods, the first sight she saw was Fortune Hill. On its top, the saltbox house stood out black with sharp edges like a cardboard cutout.

Mama's voice, faint and thin, was calling her name from the yard. By the time she started up the path, the calling had stopped and she heard the kitchen door closing.

Margaret and Erdine

I

At first, Margaret hid in corners. Sitting in corners, she forgot how to button and how to eat with a fork.

"She ain't used to being with other children, you see," the matron told the cook. "Her parents was old and lived in the country. Besides she got the lion's share, poor thing. They doted on her."

As the weeks in the Kimball County Children's Home came and went, then the months and the years, Margaret gradually took up the care of her small body once more. She moved about the rooms washing her face, eating her food, making her bed, and mending her clothes. But when she had time to herself, she still hunted corners where she curled up with her books or her thoughts. Tightly-squeezed and dim and safe the corners seemed to Margaret.

"What are you sitting there for, Margaret?" the matron would call. "What are you hiding from?"

"I ain't hiding," Margaret said as the matron took her arm.

"What is it you are doing, then?"

"I'm looking at the beds."

"The point is you are to get into one of them."

"They's too many beds all alike."

"I'll tell the Board your opinion," said the matron with amiable sarcasm, chuckling to herself. She pulled the girl's nightdress down over her head.

"And all of them children in the beds . . . ."

"Well, what about them?"

"They come and they go away," Margaret said, "and they ain't got no faces only the backs of their heads laying on the pillows."

"If you'd stop hiding in corners you'd see their faces."

"I think they ain't got no faces."

"Then you're a silly goose."

"I think their faces ain't there at all."

After matron went her way, Margaret lay awake, staring at the rows of beds and she knew she was right, for not one child turned its face toward her.

It was dark in the orphanage building even when the sun was shining. The windows were small and high up. The yard outside was dust or mud according to the weather. On one side was a pump, on the other a cistern with a rotting wooden top. The fence around the yard was made of crisscrossed wire. A few wilted blades of grass grew by the posts of the gate. Beyond the fence were the houses of the village of Trent.

When Margaret was nine, Erdine Lincoln returned to the orphanage. She stepped up the front walk like royalty coming home.

"Here, kiddie!" she said to a pale small girl named Penny Brock, sliding her suitcase handle graciously into the child's thin hands. "Ain't you glad I'm back?"

"Yes," said Penny and the two little girls went around together afterward.

It was Penny crying several weeks later that brought Margaret out of her corner.

"What're you bawling for?" Margaret asked curiously after she had stood for a while in wonder watching the tears roll down Penny's face and drop off her chin into her lap where she was twisting her hands together.

"None of your beeswax," said Penny.

She had two brown braids and was narrow as a willow shoot.

"You're making a awful racket," said Margaret and she stuck her fingers into her ears.

"You just wait 'til *your* best friend don't like you no more," said Penny. "Then see what kind of racket you make, smarty pants."

The next day when Margaret came into the sleeping room she found Penny and Erdine quarreling.

"Look here, kiddie, you only brought one of my shoes. Where's the other?" Erdine exclaimed impatiently.

"I don't know."

"But I got to have it. I sent you out to fetch both. What good will one do me, you ninny?"

"I looked all around the bush where you said."

"Well, go look again."

"I can't go back now. It's my night to set table."

"Go set it then, but you'll be sorry," Erdine said with an ugly look. Penny, her big eyes teary, went to the dining room.

"Come in, kiddie," called Erdine to Margaret, smoothing her black shingled hair. "You can't imagine how I been wanting to talk to you. You think I ain't noticed you? Say, I've seen you around. I even said to Matron, 'Who is that cute little girl with the curly hair?' You can ask her if I didn't. Them's my exact words. What's your name?"

"Margaret."

"I was fooling you. I knew your name, but I wanted to hear you say it. I'm Erdine. Is your parents both dead?"

"Yes."

"You're lucky, kiddie," Erdine went on, biting at her cuticles. "My old lady is still breathing and I wish to hell she wasn't. Every time she gets married she boots me out and here I am again."

"Has she been married much?"

"My lord I think so! Yes."

"Did you know Penny before?"

"Yes. 'Bad Penny' I call her. God how she turns up and turns up. I don't care much for her. She thinks I do but I don't."

"Why not?"

"She's such a stupid little nubbin. And she's got a bad heart. She's always sick. I can't stand sick people, can you?

"But here's a secret: Penny has this great aunt that sends her presents. Last week she sent her a jointed doll with a tin head. Even its knees bend. Next spring she's going to bring her a kitten. This aunt always sends her candy and toys. That's the reason I keep her around. She's so dumb she gives them all away."

Erdine laughed in an unpleasant way, her bony shoulders heaving, her freckles standing out darkly on her white skin.

"Do you want some scent?" she asked, suddenly throwing open her suitcase upon the bed. Her movements were quick and intense and she looked round with her shiny dark eyes like a bird or a rat uncovering its nest.

"All right," said Margaret, stepping closer.

"Lean down. I'll spray you. Hold your nose or it'll make you sneeze."

There was a quick whispered sigh and the air smelt heavily of musk.

"Mmmmm. Ain't that nice?"

"Yes."

"Don't you love it?"

"Yes."

"Oh, kiddie, it's superb. But then I knew you'd say so."

"Why?"

"Because I can tell about people. It's a gift I got, this telling what people is like. I knowed you was smart as soon as I saw you. I said to Penny, 'There's a smart kid.' You ask her if I didn't. She'll tell you. Them's my exact words."

"Will you stay long this time?"

"The good Lord knows, kiddie. I want to, now you're here."

"Why?"

"You know it's because I like you. You got good taste. You know nice items when you see them. Like my scent and your ring there. Lemme see that."

Margaret started when the older girl took hold of her hand. Erdine's fingers were moist, long and limber, extraordinarily vibrant and alive. Margaret shivered at her touch.

"That's silver, ain't it? That's superb. Where'd you get that?"

"Doctor Joe Bryant brought it to me. He comes to see me sometimes."

"I like it. Sit by me at supper."

"We got to sit where they tell us."

"You think I don't know that? Say, I grew up here, kiddie. But you can sit by me if I say so. It'll be all right."

"I will, then."

The dinner bell rang and they went down together.

"I've been waiting for you," Erdine cried excitedly one afternoon as Margaret came out into the yard after lunch. "Come sit on the fence. This'll be our special place."

"All right."

"Bad Penny's in the Infirmary and I'm a little bit glad because I want to read this to you, kiddie, by yourself. It's a story I'm inventing. I'll publish it later. It's superb."

"You mean you're making it up out of your own head?"

"Yes. I make up stories all the time. I just do it like other people breathe. It's a gift I have."

"What's it about?"

"It's about a girl who's real poor. Nobody will talk to her because she's so ragged, but her mother turns out to be a movie star and her father is a king with an army and scads of precious jewels and the girl tells her father's army to kill the people who was mean to her and she and her parents ride away in their gold Cadillac car in the end. Only there's a deal more to it."

Margaret listened marveling while Erdine read out loud for the better part of an hour. She listened on many other days to many other stories.

"We're such good friends," Erdine called over one night as they lay in bed. "We'll adore one another forever, won't we?"

"Yes," said Margaret.

"No matter where we go, we'll always remember. Here's what we must do, kiddie," said Erdine suddenly sitting up in bed. "Have you got a pin?"

"No."

"Shh. Don't wake up those other sillies. Here I've got my pajama top pinned together in front where the button came off."

"Have you got the button? I'll sew it on for you tomorrow."

"All right. Now stretch out your arm."

Margaret felt Erdine's fingers lay hold of her hand and turn up the palm so that the soft, veined underside of her arm shone white. She felt a sharp pain as Erdine jabbed in the pin. A tiny plume of dark blood jetted up and spread. Erdine sat watching Margaret's arm, a deep shadow over her face. Then quickly she touched her own arm with the pin and pressed the two arms, hers and Margaret's, together.

"Your arm is so warm," Margaret said wonderingly, trembling.

"Now we're sisters, kiddie," Erdine whispered, her laughter coming in an uncontrolled gasp that was almost hysterical. "We got each other's blood in us forever."

She took her arm away and Margaret almost wept to feel it gone and her own arm cold and exposed, with the blood crusting it.

"Have you got a dollar bill?" Erdine asked.

"Yes, I have. Hid in the bottom of my clothes drawer. Doctor Joe gave it to me last Christmas.

"Fetch it here and I'll show you something. I'd use my money but I ain't got no bills. Now watch this."

Margaret watched awestruck as Erdine carefully folded the dollar precisely in half and tore it down the crease. She handed half the bill back to Margaret and retained the other half in her fingers.

"Now, she whispered, "wherever we go in this whole world and no matter how we're changed, when we meet again we must match the halves of this bill and we'll know we're true friends and blood sisters. Ain't that superb? I read that in a book."

Margaret lay awake into the night, her throbbing arm wrapped in the bed covers, watching Erdine's sleeping face.

II

On Valentine's Day, a new girl came to the Home. She was an elegant child with natural blond curls. She owned many dresses and wore silk stockings, an affectation which struck wonder into the hearts of her new comrades. She also had a father who visited her on Sundays.

Margaret, of all the children, took little notice of her, absorbed as she was with Erdine.

The children played at fox and geese in the snow. Erdine and Margaret, when they were geese together, ran until they gasped, all around and around the outer path of the circle. Sometimes Erdine was the fox and Margaret, hid among the other geese, watched the tall bony figure creeping quickly along the paths. The other geese ran squealing away around the wheel and only Margaret stayed behind, too rapt to move, and was caught.

Toward the end of February, Erdine turned moody. The freckles stood out darkly on her pale cheeks and she scarcely spoke a word to Margaret all day long. At night she turned her face away.

At lunch Margaret bent her head, with its mist of fine pale hair, close to Erdine's as she sat down in her place, murmuring,

"You ain't mad at me, are you?"

"No."

"You act like you are."

"When I don't talk, it means I'm thinking," Erdine said loftily. "It means I'm studying on certain items. I got a right to study things out, haven't I?"

"Yes."

"Well, don't pick at me, then."

"I'm not."

"Well, then, just leave me be a while. Why do you have to stand around staring at me all the time?"

"But I don't."

"Yes, you do. Just like a silly idiot. I saw you watching me have a private conversation with that new girl Bonnie Frey. You just forever stand breathing down my neck and eyeing me."

"I wanted to give you something but you never looked around."

"What?"

"Reach your hand here. Open your fingers. There. Now close them."

"Your ring? Oh kiddie, you shouldn't give me your ring. What will your doctor friend say? He'll make you get it back."

"He won't notice. If he does, I'll say it pinched me and I put it away."

"Ain't it superb?" cried Erdine. "Look at how it just fits me!"

Early in March Penny's great aunt brought her a small striped kitten.

One afternoon, finding it on the window ledge outside the dining room, Erdine raised the window and lifted the kitten in out of the snow.

"It ain't allowed in," Penny whispered, alarmed.

"Who'll know but you and me and Margaret? We're all that's here and we ain't going to tell."

"Somebody might come in."

"Don't be such a 'fraidy calf. You're always afraid."

"I'm not."

"You're afraid to sneeze or blow your nose or go to the john for fear you'll get caught in the wrong."

"What are you doing?"

"I'm going to fix this pussy a set of paper stockings. Hold it like this, on its back."

"What for?"

"You just watch. My mom used to do this to our cats at home and we died laughing at them."

"It's trying to scratch you."

"If it does, it'll wish it hadn't. Now let go."

The cat, finding itself suddenly free, sniffed in alarm at the four small rolls of paper encasing its legs. It shook one hind leg then the other but the paper, fastened in place with rubber bands, remained. The kitten walked a few steps, twitched its front feet, and began to back across the floor slowly continuing to shake its feet one at a time.

Erdine laughed until the tears stood in her eyes.

"Look, kiddie," she cried to Margaret. "Look!"

The kitten leaped straight up into the air, stiff-legged, once, twice, then a third time.

"Take them off, Erdine," Penny said. She began to whimper.

Now the kitten raced about the room bumping into the chairs and table legs, wringing its feet as it ran. Margaret could see the wind whirling snow outside while inside the small animal flew in and out of the corners.

"Oh, the poor thing! Oh the poor thing!" Penny cried, hugging her elbows to her thin body.

The door to the dining room slammed open and a crowd of children stood staring in. At the front the new girl, Bonnie Frey, with her silk hose on, gaped to see the cat now jumping high in the middle of the room.

Still kneeling, Erdine bent her face and her bony shoulders toward the door. The short black hair stood out at the nape of her neck as she and Bonnie fixed one another with their eyes.

The kitten, having managed to free itself of all but one of the rolls of paper, whisked out at the door and down the hall. The children turned and ran after it, shouting.

At night when they lay in their beds side by side, Erdine began to talk to Margaret about the new girl.

"Kiddie, she's so stuck up," she whispered lying on her side, facing Margaret in the darkness. "She thinks she's so swell, you know. Doesn't she think she's swell?"

"Yes."

"She won't even speak."

"What?"

"She holds her nose in the air and won't even say 'hello.' She passed me twice in the hall this morning and never even as much as nodded."

Margaret hardly attended to Erdine's words. She lay listening sleepily to the murmur of Erdine's voice coming to her ears across the darkness.

"She thinks she's so big because her father brings her presents every Sunday."

"Does he?"

"Yes. Last Sunday he give her a watch. A real one. It was a cheap one though."

"Is he rich?"

"He must be, kiddie. He drives this superb car. A maroon Buick sedan. He's going to take her away as soon as the court settles he can have her. Her mother's trying to get her, too."

In the moonlight reflected from the snow, Margaret could trace the shape of Erdine's face strained toward her above the sheets. She fell asleep while she still gazed at it.

In a week's time, whenever Margaret looked for Erdine, she found her walking with Bonnie. Day after day it was always the same. In a corner of the yard or in a room of the house, she came upon the black head and the yellow head bent close together.

When Margaret tried to join them, Erdine was sullen and angry until she moved on.

At bedtime one night Margaret followed Erdine into the sleeping room and watched silently while Erdine gathered up her belongings from under the bed and then began to roll up her blankets.

"Bad Penny's in the Infirmary again," Erdine remarked at last, panting from her labors. "So I'm switching beds with her. Hers is over beside Bonnie's. Look what Bonnie gimme to come sleep by her."

Erdine stuck out her arm. A small rather tarnished watch was strapped around the wrist.

"It's Bonnie's old watch, kiddie. The one she had before her dad give her the white gold one. It don't run but the jeweler said he'd fix it for a dollar."

"But don't move, Erdine. We can't talk no more if you move. I can't listen to your stories."

"I know, kiddie. I don't want to, but it's such a superb watch, I had to say I'd do it. I'll fool her though. I won't stay but a night and then I'll move back. You'll see."

But the nights stretched on and Erdine did not come back. Penny returned and slept in the bed beside Margaret.

It was several months before Margaret discovered the torn half of the dollar bill had been taken out of the bottom of her clothes drawer. She went in the evening to where Erdine and Bonnie were sitting together on Erdine's bed with the lamp shining on their heads.

"My part of the dollar's gone out of my drawer," she said so loudly that several of the girls looked around.

"Of course it is, you stupid little nubbin," Erdine cackled, throwing back her bony shoulders. "I took it myself."

"What for?"

"Why to get this watch fixed, what do you think? I paid the jeweler with our dollar. I knew you'd want me to do it. Hear? It ticks now."

She lifted up her wrist. She and Bonnie grinned at one another evilly, tickled beyond words.

"But I thought we was supposed to keep them pieces forever."

"Did you?"

"To know each other by."

"I guess I'll know you without any old torn up money," Erdine shouted with a snort of laughter. "You'll be skinny-legged and fuzzy-haired just like you are right this minute. And you can tell me because I'll be rich and beautiful."

Bonnie stared at Erdine and turned pink with strangled mirth, though she barely opened her lips in a smile.

"But we're sisters. You shouldn't have taken away my dollar because we're sisters."

"Did you believe that?"

"Yes."

"But that was a joke, kiddie," Erdine giggled. "What a silly sport you are. I just stuck your arm to watch it bleed. I never even pricked my arm at all. I simply let on."

"Give me back the dollar."

"I tell you it's gone. I spent it."

"But it was mine. My dollar. And you shouldn't have taken it because we are sisters."

"Ha. Ha. You ain't no kin of mine, kiddie. Thank the Lord."

At first Margaret thought about Erdine a lot. She woke in the night picturing Erdine's face with its dark freckles and her limber moist fingers.

When she slept again her dreams were about Erdine. She saw herself lying on the bottom of a cold sea looking up at Erdine threshing on the surface. How Erdine beat the water with her arms striving to stay afloat! Margaret longed to join her, but a darkness spread itself between Margaret on the bottom and Erdine on the surface, widening and thickening until Margaret could see Erdine no longer.

When the darkness lifted, the water lightened slowly as a windowpane clears of steam or frost and, little by little, one sees through. But Margaret always awoke before the final clearing.

III

In the early days of summer, the orphanage children ran about the yard until their legs ached. They played at baseball and kick-the-can or at jacks on the rotting cistern top. They threw off their sweaters, wiped the sweat from their eyes and stood in line at the pump to drink their bellies full of the icy water.

Penny, who was too frail to run with the others, wandered about the yard collecting straw and leaves.

"She reminds me of a trillium," Margaret said to Erdine.

"A trillium, what's that?"

"It's a wild flower that dies if you pick it."

"She looks more like a mushroom," observed Bonnie who was standing nearby.

"Her aunt moved to California and hardly sends her a stick of gum any more," Erdine said. "I can't stand sick people, can you, kiddie?"

"No," said Bonnie. "Their breath is putrid."

"What's she got over there in the corner anyhow?"

"She's got that scrawny kitten in a box."

"She's had it there all week," said Margaret. "She feeds it pieces of meat she saves off her plate at supper."

"Let's go see it," Erdine cried.

The three girls moved to where Penny squatted before an orange crate from which the cat looked up at them with wide green eyes.

"Look at that: a cat in a box!" exclaimed Erdine.

"Ug," said Bonnie. "Don't it stink!"

"It wants to be fed. Feed it something, Penny."

Penny, looking at the girls uneasily, opened her handkerchief and, taking out a piece of ground meat, dropped it into the kitten's mouth. She kept her chin pressed against her thin neck, casting her whole face downward. Her braids hung limply over her shoulder blades.

"Why, Penny, you shouldn't keep a cat shut up. It'll die," Erdine cried out, staring at the kitten with a strange excitement.

"I'll bet it's got lice," Bonnie said, recoiling from the box distastefully.

"Has it got lice, Penny? Let me see if it has."

Erdine undid the lid, flipped it back and lifted up the kitten in her moist fingers, laughing. The kitten began to open and close its mouth, mewing loudly.

"Give it here," Penny said, following after the older girl.

"I believe it has got lice. See for yourself," Erdine called and with a swift motion of her bony shoulders dropped the kitten into Bonnie's hands. Bonnie examined it gingerly and when Penny approached her, returned it to Erdine.

The two older girls repeated this hand-off several times while moving about the yard. Their eyes sought one another's with a sly look.

Penny followed after now Erdine, now Bonnie her thin face puzzled and alarmed.

"You give it here to me," she demanded.

"Is this kitten really yours, kiddie?" Erdine asked at last, pausing with the animal sprawled on her palm.

"Yes."

"Then you ought to give it to me."

"Why?"

"Because I'm your friend. I've always been your friend, haven't I?"

"Yes," Penny said, stopping confusedly and staring at the kitten.

"Well, you're supposed to give presents to your friends. Can I have it?"

"No."

"But I'm so good to you. I came to see you in the Infirmary, didn't I? And I gave you some scent?"

"Yes."

"Well, then, you should give me this cat."

"I want it."

"If you won't give it to me, give it to Bonnie. She's your friend too. She'd like to have a cat," cried Erdine dropping the furry creature into Bonnie's open hand.

"No."

"Then give it to me. Will you? Please? Pretty please?"

Penny stared at Erdine. "All right," she whispered at last.

"Then here's what I'll do with it since you gave it to me and it's mine," Erdine cried out in a transport of triumph and she snatched the kitten from Bonnie and ran away across the yard with Penny, Bonnie, and Margaret following after her. They saw Erdine run up to the cistern. She knelt, jerked up one of the weathered boards and let the kitten drop inside.

The three girls stood gaping. Margaret moved closer and peered down into the dark hole.

"Why did you do that?" Bonnie cried out, loud with excitement.

"Because it was lousy," Erdine said, her voice choked.

The two older girls stared at one another over the cistern top.

Bonnie watched Erdine's fingers, which had held the kitten, with an intense fascination.

Penny, kneeling, gazed down into the cistern, looking for the kitten. She turned to Erdine, beginning to snuffle.

"Get it back," she said.

It was too much for Erdine and Bonnie. They ran away whooping with laughter.

Margaret, however, stayed behind. She knelt and ripped a board from the cistern top, then another and another until she had made a hole large enough for her body to pass through.

She let herself down into the cistern, hung for a moment at the rim taking a breath, then pushed herself under the black water. She groped about until her lungs ached and her senses spun. When she had given the kitten up, her fingers closed round it.

Rising with it through the darkness, she was conscious first of the bright sky, then of a dimness falling across her face, the shadow of Penny's head where she sat on a corner of the cistern, waiting.

Nativity

I

"So your girl jilted you, Bobby?" Mrs. Proctor asked.

"Yes, Mama."

By sheer effort of will Robert kept his voice steady and stood watching her continue to pack tomatoes into glass jars as if he'd told her the springing cow had calved or the mail would be late out from town.

Beside them on the stove the canner seethed and bubbled. Robert threw the letter on the table. He was tall and heavy-shouldered with unkempt hair that stood on his head in tufts. The only sound in the room was the popping of jar lids. Mrs. Proctor looked over at the letter. Then he saw her gaze slide to the jars she had just lifted out of the canner where they stood in an immaculate row reflected in the surface of the sinkboard. He knew by the way her mouth moved that she was counting them.

Beyond the tomatoes, ranged along the wall, were other canned foods grouped according to kind. She had been the summer putting them up. There was a row of peaches, the golden halves perched on one another in erect broad-shouldered quarts. Glasses filled with grape jelly were stoppered neatly with paraffin. Watermelon pickles lay murky and insular bottled in green glass. The depths of all the jars shone with cold restrained colors like gems.

After she had checked them over, Mrs. Proctor picked up the letter and looked at it through the bottoms of her spectacles.

"She's made up her mind," she said. "You'd best go back to school without seeing her at all. You'll be dropped if you stay away."

"She's got no right to break off."

"No. But being a Lennox, she doesn't care, you see. Her father's the same. He's got no feel for duty and no idea of getting on in the world. He serves me just so with the land he farms for me. He'll go miles off to preach at a revival when the corn should be planted."

"Meg promised to marry me when I finished school," Robert said. "I'll hold her to it."

"You can't as she's no sense of keeping her word. They're an immoral bunch, I say. No pride in what they own or the work they do. How can you make pledges with people like that? You'd best let her go and count it good luck. It was a bad match from the start. I said so. Her sort can't do for themselves. Nine children hungry and the father off preaching gratis. He's an educated man, you know. Still, he's content to do other folks' farming. There's not a whole stick of furniture in the house though I've given them nice pieces and so have others."

"She's going as a missionary to Africa," Robert said. "She'll be poor as dirt."

"Only a Lennox would do it."

Robert made no answer. Thinking of the letter, he felt his neck and face flush. He breathed through his mouth.

"She's not worth the spit off your tongue," his mother said. "Not a fit wife for a professional man as you'll be. You go back to college now, Bobby. It's better left as it is."

A breeze sprang in at the kitchen window pressing back the curtain and ruffling the feathers of the canary in its cage so that it shook itself.

"Ah, Biddy, has the wind brushed you?" said Mrs. Proctor. She reached up and shut the window half way.

She set the last jars of tomatoes into the canner, lifting them expertly with the tongs. The heat off the steaming water reddened her broad face so that she and the cans were much of a color. She stood at the sink counting the jars.

The canary peeped, hopped a little way, and began anxiously pecking at the perch.

"You want seeds, do you?" said Mrs. Proctor in a high falsetto, condescending to the bird and faintly jeering. "But you know you are far too fat already," she cried. "You care for nothing but seeds now that you've lost your song. You're grown big as a chicken where once you were slender. You're so old it's clear I must make an end of you soon. You haven't sung these three months."

She gave the bird a dipper of seed and turned back to her son.

"Go to college," she urged. "Go along. Go along. It's better that you part from her."

"I can't."

"But hadn't you as well have done with her?" his mother persisted. "The girl's got strange ways. I saw it from the first. She didn't want you as a husband only, she wanted the soul out of your body. She knew at last she wouldn't have it and now she's gone off. Isn't that the way of it?"

Robert ground his teeth.

"You go back and finish your course. She'll be sorry when you're a graduate veterinarian, I promise you," his mother said. "When you're a great success treating pet dogs and cats, for that's where the money lies, when you have an office with a glass door in the town and money to plant this farm to grain full acreage, then she'll see her mistake."

Robert put his fingers violently through his hair.

"I'm damned if I can let her go!" he said.

They heard a step.

"Here's Meg now, come up the field," Mrs. Proctor said. "You'll settle it between you."

"Where is she?"

"On the porch."

"Why doesn't she knock?"

"She will. She must always stroke the cat first."

A silence held the room. Then the footsteps began again and a rapid light knock was heard at the door. The knob turned gently and the girl stood on the threshold, pale and slender, holding a shawl around her face.

"Sit down, Meg," Mrs. Proctor said, indicating a chair at the kitchen table.

"Eh, Robert, are you come home?" the girl cried out in a low voice, seating herself.

"How are you, Meg?" he asked her.

"I'm well, thank you, Robert. I've brought the rent, Mrs. Proctor."

"I'm obliged. And how's your family keep?"

"Ma's back hurts her. I'll do her milking tonight."

"And so you're off on a ship, Meg?" Mrs. Proctor continued, beginning to scrub off the table. "When is it to be?"

"Two weeks a Thursday."

"What does your father say about your going?"

"Pa says, 'God's will be done.' The people have a great need."

"Your life'll be changed."

Mrs. Proctor turned away to the cleaning up. Robert sat looking down at his shoe.

"I was sorry to send you such a letter, Bob," Meg said, fixing him with her dark steady eyes. "You know I'd rather have told you and us sitting face to face like we are now. Are you going back to college soon?"

"No."

"Why, what are you planning to do then?" cried his mother swinging around on him in exasperation.

But Robert got up without answering, walked to the window and stood looking out with his back to the kitchen. The rest of Meg's visit, he stood there unable to make himself speak to her. When the girl went away he watched her cross the field down through the cattle, her black shawl bold against the green pasture and flapped over her shoulders.

In the afternoon Robert walked out over the place. The house was made of brick and had had the first plastered walls in the county and later the first plumbing and the first electric wiring. There was a chicken yard in use to the right of the house and a pig pen behind. The truck garden lay to the left and down the slope. The house was built on a hill like a castle and all the fields rolled from it: here second cutting hay, there corn, there soybeans, pasture fields, and the brown tilled acres where winter wheat was sprouting.

The dairy barn was painted red. During his lifetime, Robert's father kept a fine large herd of Jersey cattle which he, the father, had loved. Now the stanchions were only partially filled at milking time.

Robert knew his mother looked forward to the day he would come home from college and tear down the dairy barn to make room for storage bins. She wished to put the farm entirely to grain. Grain prices were high while milk brought in little money. She had pestered his father to get rid of the cattle. It was the one thing he had denied her.

Robert moved into the pasture field among the cattle. He ran his eye over each animal as was his habit, calculating poundage, condition, stage of lactation, and market value.

He stamped morosely among the beasts slapping now this one now that one on the rump until they gave way before him.

A part of the herd was young heifers but a number of the original cows still remained. They were tamer than the rest. By the way they crowded around him, he recognized them as the old cows which had known his father.

The hides of these cattle were dappled and they were delicately made, superb dairy types with dish faces. While Robert marked the veining of the udders and the setting of the tailbones, unwillingly he became conscious of their eyes.

The irises were brown and translucent so that he looked beneath them at shadings of violet and flecks of white. Lying deep back was an area of secret awareness. They remembered his father. He was sure of it. They stood trembling, staring at him with their curious, deep eyes.

II

During the afternoon Meg leaned to shake a rug from an upstairs window of the tenant house. She glanced over the countryside and her sharp eyes found Robert among the cattle. Her pulse quickened at the sight for she sensed in him a raptness that startled and bemused her. It was as if she saw another man, hidden in Robert's body until now, come out and stand before her. He raised his head and looked at her. She lifted her hand. Then each turned quickly away feeling somehow caught out in a secret by the other.

Meg continued with the housework. She watched her own quick, slim fingers make up the beds, sweep the floors, wash the children and every moment, plain as the sight of her own working hands, the figure of Robert stood on the outer rim of her consciousness as she had seen him standing in the pasture field.

Meg helped get supper and feed the younger children. Her mother was daily overburdened with work. There was constant cooking, scrubbing, sewing, and ironing to be done. Meg, as the eldest girl, kept her fingers flying doing for the young ones. Still, the time was fast coming when they would be able to do for themselves.

Evening shadows stretched across the land. The wind dropped. Meg, with her shawl tied round her waist, carrying several buckets, stepped out of the house and walked through the fields.

She slowly climbed the hill following a dusty cow path. As far off as she could see, the fields of beans and corn continued. She walked through pasture land yellowing now in the hot dry end of summer but lush and wide still. On the slope nearest her, the chickens were scattered like pieces of white paper.

There was the Proctor house, there the hay barn, the machine shed, the silo, the corn bins, the dairy barn, all she'd looked on every day of her life. Now she was going away. In all likelihood, she would never see them again. Nor would she see Robert, whose presence she felt everywhere.

She could leave the farm without a backward look. Robert was another matter. It was as if, now, walking to the barn, she felt his fingers twined with hers as they'd been more often than not through the years. By Bob's side, she'd known who she was. Apart from him, who on God's earth would she be?

In the dairy barn, Meg set down her buckets and tucked up her skirt before she saw Robert standing watching her from the shadows.

"You'll not get on that boat," he said.

She saw that he was trembling.

"Bob, I've got to go."

"You gave your word to me. You can't go back on it."

Meg, standing in the transparent dusk of the milking parlour, felt the sweet breath of the cows about her. Now and then one or another of them moved its head, knocking its horns against the stanchion.

"I think, Bob," she said gently, frowning, "our love was a shallow sort."

"No!"

"Listen won't you? You'll see I'm right. It was such a young feeling. It was ourselves we loved, not each other. It's better to cut loose from that."

She saw he did not hear anything of what she said. She knew he couldn't endure her to win over him even as it had been when they were children.

He laid hold on her, lifting her to him. His fingers bruised her so that she rested heavily against him, turned giddy by the pain.

"You'll marry me," he brought out, almost beyond speaking. "I'll see to it!"

He pressed against her, pushing his mouth onto hers. She jerked back. They struggled, stumbling, to the back of the milking parlour behind the cattle where she lost her footing and went down on the floor in the straw and dung. He knelt over her, big as a mountain, strong as a bull. She caught his breath on her face, hot and rapid, filling her nostrils and her mouth.

Scrambling and sliding, she got to her feet, pulling herself up along the wall. He snatched at her clothes. She ducked in among the cattle who were moving about uneasily, lifting their heads now and then to bellow. He caught at her hair as she flung open the door and ran out into the barn lot.

Across the field she could see the headlights of her father's truck standing by the hay rick. She started toward it, walking a little dizzily, with her head down. She could hear Robert trudging doggedly after her through the blackening dusk.

III

Meg's father came to meet them, swinging the lantern at his side, lighting his feet.

"There's a cow down and can't get up," he said. "She's calving but there's something amiss. Listen."

They stood quiet. After a while they heard the cow bellow. They found her lying on her side at the edge of the pasture. She was big with calf and in bitter misery trying to give birth. Her eyes were wide and glassy. She looked toward them, not registering their presence, knowing only her own self, the agony of her need. Robert realized she had been trying to calve a long time.

He threw off his shirt, twisted it around her neck and kicked and pulled her onto her feet. She grunted, lurched, went to her knees. He whacked her rump and she struggled up once more.

"Hold her," Robert said, handing the shirt to Lennox.

Meg stepped up and gripped the twisted shirt, placing her hands beside her father's. The cow strained forward, half-falling. Between them they held her steady. Her breathing was harsh and painful.

Robert plunged his hand and arm up to the shoulder into the cow's body along the birth canal. The cow lunged forward and bellowed hoarsely.

"Now, dammit, hold her," Robert cried.

Meg and her father leaned their weight against the cow's head and chest. The creature's breath smelt of soured hay. She groaned while they twisted the shirt in their hands, Meg at one side, her father at the other. Robert struggled against the cow's contracting muscles, his face, his chest and back dripping with sweat. The veins stood out on his forehead as he worked to touch the calf. At last he felt it but only the tail bone.

The position was wrong, then. He would have to turn the calf to bring the back legs out. The headlights of the truck shone on his naked shoulders as he strained at the work.

"Is there a hay bale in the truck?" he panted.

"Yes," Lennox answered. "I came out to feed."

"I need bale twine."

When Meg ran to get the twine, the cow tried to lie down. Robert and Lennox fought to keep her up. Robert took the twine from Meg and looped it with his teeth and the fingers of his free hand.

He rocked the calf with all his strength. His arm in the birth canal was numb. He heaved again, grunting with the effort.

He believed he would never turn the calf. He pushed, his face blanching, his breath rasping in his throat. Push, rest, push again.

At last he was able to bring up the feet into his cramped fingers and to fasten the twine to them. He began to pull strongly, bracing his feet and throwing his whole weight against the calf's legs. He continued pulling hard, leaning back. One piece of twine broke and Robert fell back, staggering. Then he must work to place fresh twine on and pull again.

When at last he got the legs straightened, he cried, "Let her loose."

Meg and Lennox relaxed their hold and the cow stumbled, floundered forward and went down, bellowing. Robert went down with her and lay behind her gently bringing out the calf, letting the cow push and pulling along with her in a strange shared rhythm. He relaxed in his efforts, ceasing to force his will on the cow. He let her have her way, only helping her as he could.

It seemed to him the strange exalted pulling would go on forever. His arm throbbed somewhere far off from himself, not a part of him any longer. The cow groaned and her muscles, as she pushed on the calf, ground his arm against her pelvic bone.

He scarcely connected the sensation with his own body. He pulled on in a dream, bathed in a deep yearning. Robert wanted the calf to come. He pulled and wanted to bring the calf out alive. Aching, with a quiet longing, he pulled, groaning along with the cow, and slowly the calf began to come.

An inch, two inches, the hind legs, the hocks. The front legs were out, the head. Robert lay back in a pool of greenish putrid afterbirth holding the dark wet calf. At once he scrambled to his feet and jerked the calf up by its hind legs, lifting it clear of the ground so that its full length dangled in the air and shook it until the mucus ran from its mouth. After a little, it snorted, coughed and began to shiver.

He set it down.

"It's alive!" cried Lennox hoarsely. "I saw it breathe."

Robert laughed weakly and leaned against the truck. The cow lay at his feet, exhausted but at peace.

A warmth settled over Robert's shoulders. He knew Meg had thrown his shirt over him but he did not look at her or speak. He was too content. All his rage was dissolved away.

He came to himself suddenly to discover Meg's face, pale in the cowl of her dark hair, looking up into his. He divined that time had elapsed without his knowing. He felt she had spoken to him but he had been unconscious of her words.

"What?" he said.

"As Father's gone to milk the cows, I'll go along home now," she repeated haltingly.

"I'll walk you down."

He moved beside her, putting on his shirt. He had begun to chill as the night air touched his wet body. He smelt of the stinking afterbirth. The skin of his arms and chest were stiff with it. He thought of a hot bath, clean clothes. As they walked along in silence, gradually his shivering grew less.

They stepped from the darkness of the fields into the strong beam of the yard light.

"What is it you're thinking of?" Meg asked him as she had used to do when they were children. He found her sharp gaze on him.

"I was thinking," he answered, "that if you must go, then you must."

"I'll pump some water for you to wash," she said.

"It'll wait till I get home."

But she said, "Lean over and cup your hands."

She began to push down the pump handle. It took all her effort. He watched her as she panted and strained to bring up the water. The ridges and knots of her muscles were strange to him and her breath that came in grunts of effort. At last the water flowed in a pure gush.

He stripped away his shirt once more and plunged his hands into the cold clear water. It made him tremble but he welcomed the icy flushing. He ducked his head under the pump. The water sluiced over his shoulders and back and down his arms. He threw back his head, flinging the water from his eyes, and laughed aloud.

She gave him her shawl to dry himself. He swept back his hair with his fingers and put on his shirt, buttoning it about his throat and over his chest. He took up a stick and scraped the mud from his shoes. Then he leant forward and drank from the pump, holding his mouth to the last trickling stream as she stood on the platform, her skirts flapping around her like wings, braiding up her hair.

On Gobbler's Knob

Up on top of the world I saw Boann on her wedding day. She was drunk on blackberry wine lying flat on the warm ground with the morning mist rising from her shoulders.

She grew up out of the tangled vines like the beginning of all things. Her mouth was wide and smiling and stained purple. She was a big tow-headed girl and soft white hairs grew down the back of her neck and on her arms. She threw back her head and laughed up from deep inside her body until the wet soil shook. She bowed her head and pressed her mouth against the earth as if she were telling it secrets about the day it was going to die.

The dummy led us to her. Roy, that came to Kimball County with the revivalist and passed the plate for him in his tent. Roy knew where she was and for a nickel and two dimes he showed us.

He was first on top and his old yellow hound dog was second. Roy stood on the knob slobbering and grinning the way he always did, making sounds that were giggles instead of words and watching the men tramp up to where she was lying.

They were dressed in black as if they had come to hang her. They were fighting mad. I was with them, not mad but hopeful.

When the men were all on top of the knob, they stood sweating in the deep July morning and staring at Boann because they'd never seen anything like her. I stood where I could see her face when they told her.

E. M. Tussey, a barber from Powdertown, set his feet wide and hacked in his throat.

"You there," he said.

She raised her head and looked at him and through him off among the floating black mountain tops.

"She's stupid drunk," said a storekeeper from Kinny Ridge and spat among the sassafras.

"We want to know where's Georgie?" said Tussey heavily.

"Georgie," she said and it wasn't a name or a question but more like a hymn like "Rock of Ages" or "Lead Kindly Light."

"She's drunk," someone said again.

Boann sat up. Her dress was dew-streaked and her shoes were gone. Still she looked like King Solomon's queen.

"I don't know where Georgie is," she said. She started to twist up her hair and clear drops of water squeezed out of it and ran over her cheek.

"God, girl, you married him this morning, didn't you?" Tussey bawled. "You must know."

She nodded.

"I married him on this spot when the new moon set in the dark this morning. He's still here. All you got to do is look for him. Georgie's rolled up in the sun. He's jumping over the rocks in the waterfall where we swum in the dark. He's tangled in my hair."

"My God Almighty, she's soused to the eyebrows."

"These hill people is lunatic anyway."

Boann stood up. She was half a head taller than any man of us.

"The part of Georgie you're looking for is gone off somewhere," she said agreeably and started to walk away.

It hurt me to look at her. She was the Song of Songs. She was a sweet savour, a garden, a honeycomb, a roe. But she turned me into stone. It had been like that since we were children. I couldn't talk to her. I could talk to anybody but not to her. I loved her and I couldn't tell her. When she looked at me my tongue withered and slid down my throat.

But I kept coming back every summer. Even after my parents were divorced and the summer place was sold I came back. This year I came too late. Boann was in love with a revivalist. Still, I had one last hope.

"Tell her," I said, "about Georgie."

Tussey coughed somewhat to loosen his throat. "Boann —"

She stopped.

"Us men is from all around the country where Georgie's been preaching. And we —"

She stood with one finger in the neck of the wine bottle, waiting.

"This Georgie of yours is a —" Tussey blurted and stopped. The tone of his voice was not pleasant. Boann didn't move but she wasn't drunk any more.

"He's God's man."

"He ain't. He —," the storekeeper from Kinny Ridge started to say but Tussey cut in, putting it off.

"How long you knowed him, girl?"

She smiled with her mouth open. "I've knowed Georgie since the hills was hot as fire and the world steaming in the sky. I've knowed Georgie since the big ferns grew here and things muttered in the mud. And before that."

"People say she went to the revival meeting for the first time last week," I said.

"Who looks after her? She ain't twenty yet, I'll be bound," Tussey said to me. "She don't know about Georgie. That's plain."

Boann sat down cross-legged on the ground with her chin in her palm. "I seen Georgie first up there at the preaching. He was saying 'Sweet Jesus' and the glory was on him. His sweat was dark like blood."

"The people was talking and drowsing and they hadn't caught hold but I seen it. I stood up and I walked down the dirt path inside the tent. In there was scalding hot and the lamps beating and I stood alone up from the people and I felt Hallelujah and I felt Amen. It didn't come to me shouting but quiet and calm and that was the second time."

"She's lunatic religious."

"She don't see what you mean, Tussey."

But I felt down-hearted because I knew now Georgie was mixed up with the religiousness that was so strong in her.

"Did you ask the dummy here, Georgie's pal, where Georgie is at?" the storekeeper said to Tussey.

"He just shakes his head," Tussey answered shortly.

"What's that Roy doing outside a institution is what I want to know," a banker from Cephas whispered to me. "There is a real lunatic. He's certainly a escaped booby. He ain't got no sense at all, near as a body can tell."

I looked over at Roy. He was petting his hound like he'd lost interest in Tussey and the rest.

Boann's face was stiff. She didn't move. She was beginning to distrust us.

"For Chrissake tell her," I said. I wanted to see it.

"Where's your kin, girl?" said Tussey, hedging.

Boann stood up. "What about Georgie? What do you want him for?"

She stared at me. She was turning hostile. But I wanted them to tell her, not me.

"Her grandpap raised her. He died last spring," I answered Tussey. "That hill giant with the long white hair and back straight as a boy at eighty. Seven feet tall wasn't he, Boann?"

"And two inches more. A better man than you, Billy Watt."

She was absolutely angry now.

"He was a fine old giant," I told Tussey. "His talk was worth something to hear. He taught Boann more than I learned in college: ballads and tales and the Bible. He taught her to hunt nights. He brought her up in the fear of God and honest as a saint. That's why she'll hand you Georgie once she knows the truth about him."

I thought about the old man. Our vacation cabin was next to his farm. I used to help that giant clear off his fields and heap the brush in the front yard where he burnt it. He was a man safe and sure of himself. He farmed in the old way. His land was what he cared for. And Boann. "You look after her, Billy Watt," he said.

I could see him. And I wanted more than life to keep talking until I understood certain things about him. But the men grew impatient.

"All this ain't getting us nowhere," said the storekeeper from Kinny Ridge. "We got to find this Georgie and fast before he—"

"What I was driving at," said Tussey, "is ain't she got no house where she lives in?"

"Grandpap's farmhouse, but she doesn't live in it much."

"What I'm driving at," said Tussey, "is maybe Georgie is at her place."

"At that he might be," agreed the storekeeper. "Might be he—."

"He's already skipped out with our money if you want my opinion," offered the banker from Cephas.

They were getting closer and closer to saying it.

"Did you ever see Georgie have much money on him?" the banker asked Boann.

"Who wants to know?"

I knew her. She was deciding to throw us all down off of Gobbler's Knob.

"Better tell her," I said.

The men looked sidelong at one another. Boann walked in among us and stood above us. Her face was black.

"You," she said and took hold of Tussey's coat. "You say it."

Tussey tried to back off but she held him fast. He didn't say anything for quite a while. Then he told her.

"Georgie is a crook," he said.

"Who says that?"

"We all do," said two of the other men together, angry now and determined.

"He's talked you blind, girl, like he done us, is all," said the banker and he was bitter. "He come into our towns preaching the glory road and stole us poor."

Still she wouldn't understand.

"He spoke on the Barranquilla missionaries," Tussey told her. I saw she remembered that. "He took up collection for them every preaching. He got private donations besides. We found out there ain't no Barranquilla Missionaries. All that coin goes into Georgie's pockets and the dummy's."

Boann dropped the wine bottle. After a minute she said, "If it's money you want, I got money. Grandpap left me money in the bank. I'll get it out and I'll put it in the desk drawer in the parlour. It'll be there at sundown. You can help yourselves. You can take all you want and leave Georgie be."

"It ain't so much the money," said one man very gently. He had not spoken before. "We don't like to be fooled is the very main consideration."

"We're going to find Georgie and take back any of our money he's got left," explained Tussey flatly. "Then we're going to tar and feather that revivalist and ride him out on a rail."

Two of the younger men took off their hats, slapped their legs with them and called out "amen." It was supposed to be a mimic of the way Georgie did it. It was a mistake. Boann picked up the wine bottle and hit one of them over the head with it. He set off down Gobbler's Knob and the rest of us broke and ran too.

Boann didn't follow us. I was so disappointed I ached. I dropped behind the men trotting down the knob. When they were out of sight among the trees, I sat down to wait for Boann. I had things to say to her when she was calmer. When she figured out for herself that it was true about Georgie, she'd come down and help run him out of the country. If that happened: if, please God, that only happened, then I'd talk to her. Somehow, for the first time I'd talk to her and tell her how I felt.

I sat low and hidden away in a clump of sassafras seedlings and chewed on the slippery leaves. From that spot on the side of the knob, I could see most of Grandpap's farm.

How it would have hurt him to find those briars and burdocks in his cornfields. And the barn, door sagging open, empty of cows. And the brush heap mouldy and low and gone unkindled for years. The house itself had a dead look of blank windowpanes and loose shingles.

It was curious how my hands itched to hoe those fields, not so much to redeem the wasted land as to follow some idea blown out of the old man's living brain that still hung like the mist over the hill fields in the year after his death.

Not for the first time I thought of staying on the farm. If only Boann and I could have lived there together. If only I could have described my soul to her one of those summer nights we hunted over the fields, it might have been me instead of Georgie. God knows one night she showed me her soul.

It was a night we had the dogs with us. Their eyes shone like quick-silvered quarters in the lantern light. That night was drunk, rocking around us warm as a hug. The black was shot with moonlight like steel in the ocean, heavy and relucent, drifting down and down to coat the ground.

Boann was excited. She was always listening. I could see the strong silvered muscles in her neck as she leaned forward. But she wasn't listening to the dogs or the tree frogs but to something else around her and inside her. We both listened.

The farther we went the more excited she became. I could hear her quick light breathing. The night picked Boann up in its fingers and stroked her and she listened to it talk.

We had been walking along the top of a hill with the dogs not hunting much but sticking tight to us wondering together about the dark. Then I fell and broke the lantern. We were following a cow path into woods so dense we couldn't see a foot before us.

Boann went on ahead. But soon she stopped and spread her hands back to stop me and the dogs. When I came up to her I saw that she was trembling and I looked over her shoulder. The ground dropped away sheer into nothing perhaps five inches from the toes of her shoes.

"Jesus Almighty!" I said.

But she was staring straight ahead smiling with her mouth open. She took off her shoes and threw them over the cliff and we heard them hit rock faint and far away minutes later.

Boann tore off her belt and threw that over the cliff too.

"Oh sweet Lord God I feel so funny. I feel Your fingers on my shoulder. I felt His fingers on my shoulder, Billy, so I stopped. I want to rest my head in the people's lap because God is splitting out of it. I want to put on white and go into the cities for a prophet."

There were words I should have said to her then but all I could think of was the city where my home was and of my home itself: that flat-roofed suburban cell stuck on the face of the Zoning Committee's earth, that noxious split-level fungus, that mushroom among the thousand mushrooms. A TV, a family room, a bar, cafe curtains, a barbecue rotisserie. And my parents talking. "If it wasn't for the goddamned taxes, last year I'd have netted—." "And Madge found this marvelous psychoanalyst who told her it isn't her fault Harry's a mess. It's entirely due to his Aunt Amy and the years he lived in Medicine Hat—."

Of a sudden Boann took hold of my hand and said, "You come with me, Billy. We'll go together, the two of us, and save the people."

And I wanted to shout, "Yes, by god! I'll go with you."

But I knew after we'd been to them and gone they would mention us at a cookout or at cocktails-and-buffet and say, "But that's hardly what I had in mind." And I thought that if I tried to save the people I'd lose myself and I was afraid to let go of myself and say yes. And so instead I laughed in her face like she'd cracked a joke. She stiffened and stared at me. Then the dogs treed and we ran off to find them.

That fall I went home and began to spend some time in my father's business where I was sick in the men's room nearly every day. I thought about Boann incessantly. I thought of her as my one chance in a million for escape. Still, I wouldn't let myself quit right away. Because the funny thing is, I was good at the business. I seemed to make all the right moves by instinct. Profits came dropping down like the rain falling. All I had to do was catch them. So I stayed until I salted away enough to start out on my own and then I left.

But by the time I got back to Kimball County, Grandpap was dead and Boann was married and my chance in a million was gone. It wasn't until I heard about Georgie being a crook that I thought it might be possible I'd get a second chance.

It was late afternoon before Boann came down from Gobbler's Knob stepping light as a deer. She didn't stop or look at me when I stood up from the seedlings but it was plain she'd known I was there. You couldn't fool her.

I followed her home. I wanted to talk to her but the set of her back worried me. Finally I hurried up behind her and reached my hand out to touch her but just then we came in sight of the house and we saw Georgie.

One look and I knew it was the revivalist. Georgie was lying with his back against the brush heap, his hands cupped under his head. He was young and not very big. He looked about twelve years old except his body was broad and powerfully built. I thought he was asleep but he wasn't. He was letting the fine mist of rain that was falling wash his face.

Boann walked through the gate and sat down beside him. The rain mist gathered in her hair and the westering sun shined through it. Boann smiled and Georgie smiled but they didn't look at one another.

I was disappointed again. I had hoped when they met they would argue. I wanted to hear her accuse him and hear him admit it but nothing like that happened. Still, instead of leaving, I waited because

I knew the men would come. When they called Georgie to his face, Boann would have to believe it. Then surely she would turn to me, and that would be the time to tell her how I felt.

I didn't like to look at Boann and Georgie while I waited so I closed my eyes. When finally I heard the men coming and opened my eyes everything was pink: the sun was pink behind pink clouds. The sky and the grass were pink.

The sun set quickly. The rain had stopped but heat thunder drummed on the hills. The glow that grew up out of the west turned out to be men carrying torches. They wound up through the dark valley muttering like the thunder. Gobbler's Knob was still pink at the top and seemed to be floating. In the yard the air was smothering hot like sticking your face into a felt hat.

And there stood Boann and Georgie like two fools not even looking toward the men, not paying them any mind at all.

"Yonder comes Tussey and the rest to tar and feather Georgie," I said.

But Boann had her mind otherwise directed. There she stood and stretched up her two arms into the air.

"Billy, you'll laugh," Boann said, "but when I'm beside of Georgie like this, I can reach up my hands and touch God's face full of soft wrinkles.

"I can feel the Spirit flowing down my arms like boiling water. I can feel it and I can tell Georgie I feel it and he knows what I mean."

Before I could answer her back, the men came into the yard. I saw Boann in the torch light, her eyes glistening. Georgie was smiling at her. He didn't even turn to look at the men when they spewed into the yard.

He hardly looked at them even when Tussey walked up, grabbed his shirt and ripped it off his shoulders. Seven or maybe eight of the men were already gathering sticks on the slope below the yard. They brought the sticks up and dumped them on the brush heap. They were war-whooping like Indians. They threw lighted torches onto the pile.

"Where at's our money, preacher?" Tussey said, drunk as a lord.

The men joggled in, elbowing and rough. They pushed Boann away from Georgie. They took Georgie in their hands and threw him onto the ground.

I watched Boann. Now she would see Georgie was really a thief. The men had the feathers in burlap sacks. They had a bucket of tar. I thought Georgie would yell but he didn't. He didn't do anything. Boann was standing at the edge of the yard staring off into the woods.

She was watching for something. She was listening, too. And all this time she never glanced at Georgie. Before long I saw she heard what she was listening for. I strained my ears but all I could hear was the men shouting and a dog whining and yelping around at the back of the farmhouse.

The perspiration beaded out on my upper lip and on my forehead cold as icewater. Boann was playing some little game of her own and had been all along and I had missed it.

Right away she walked off toward the house. She moved so fast I was scarcely sure where she went but I ran into the dark musty house in time to hear her bare feet pat across the front room and into the parlour. Still standing in the doorway I made the big effort.

"Boann," I said, "now they've nabbed Georgie and you see he's a sure enough crook, I want to say—."

But she was playing some little game of her own. She lit the gas mantle in the parlour. It caught and she stood with one arm raised turning it up. The light licked down her arm and spread into her face. It lit up not only Boann but also a man standing in the middle of the parlour floor.

"I been waiting for you, Roy," Boann said, never looking toward me at all.

Roy wet his big hanging-open lips with his pink tongue and stared at her. While both of them stood there not saying anything, Roy's yellow hound dog pushed a hole in the rotten screen of the kitchen door and came in, whining. Boann didn't move but after a while Roy took a step toward the back door.

"Out front," Boann said, "they're fixing to tar and feather Georgie."

All the time Roy was smiling this very vacant smile.

"They're drunk enough they might kill Georgie," Boann said.

Roy smiled. I could hear Boann breathing. Roy began to work his mouth but no sound came. His chin got wet. The dog pawed his legs and whined. After a long time of this, Roy turned toward the back door.

"I got to tell you these few things, Roy," Boann said.

Roy stopped and licked his lips again. He stood motionless with his back toward Boann.

"You think I'm dumb," said Boann. "I ain't. I know something has got hold of Georgie. I've knowed it for a long time. He's easy led. I know that, too. But now it's me that's got hold of him, Roy. I got my hold this morning. He knowed and I knowed. I'm telling you the truth."

Roy turned around, still smiling.

Boann's voice went hoarse. "Georgie's let go of you, Roy," she said, "and now I'm telling you to turn loose of him."

She brought out the last three words very slow. Roy rubbed his bleary blue eyes with the heel of his hand. Then he put both his hands behind his back and worked his mouth, making no sound.

"I know you can talk," Boann told him very quietly. "I've knowed you ain't no dummy for a long time."

Roy, standing with his hands behind his back, stopped smiling.

"Your dog knows you can talk, Roy," Boann said. "That yeller hound keeps whining up into your face. Why? Because you talk to him when you're alone. He can't understand what's wrong with you, you don't say nothing now.

"When Georgie's with you a long time and then with me, I can tell you been talking to him. I can sort your ideas out of his head like pinching rotten apples.

"You ain't no idiot, either. I've seen your eyes when you look at money. Talking about money, that's how come you're here this minute. You're come after Grandpap's money I told them men I'd put in the desk drawer. There ain't none. I made it up."

"The Great God damn you then," Roy screeched out: pow! like an explosion, "and all your kin, you long-legged Jesus-loving hill witch!"

And he kept on, using words strong as the smell of old blood. He piled them up on Boann. He had a knife in the hand he took from behind his back.

Boann didn't look at it. "The reason I waited for you to come back," she went on to say to him calmly, "is to tell you, find yourself another meal ticket. You know me and you know I mean what I say. Turn him loose."

Roy didn't look sleepy any more. His eyes weren't bleary but wide open and wicked as hell. He jumped Boann with the knife. The blade missed but his weight threw her down full length on the floor.

While I dived into the parlour and on top of Roy I was thinking over and over like a cracked record: 'All the time there wasn't any more hope than there is snow in hell; up or down Gobbler's Knob, never any hope at all.'

And while I beat Roy on the head, I laughed because the whole thing was such a goddamned crazy joke on me. Roy dropped his knife when I landed on him but now under my fingers his shoulders heaved up in an ocean roll and I fell off onto the floor.

"Roy."

It was Boann's voice. She was standing in the kitchen doorway. She sounded very calm. I thought it would be nice if she started screaming for help but she didn't. Roy hesitated, kneeling on the floor, looking up at her.

"They're getting ready to tar and feather Georgie," Boann said. "Out in front. They're going to heat up the tar. They're building a fire on the old brush heap."

Roy lunged up off the floor like a sprinter and out through the front room without stopping. Boann stood with her arms folded on her chest. I got to my feet and watched, my knees shaking. We heard Roy throw open the front door. Outside air blew out the gas mantle in the parlour.

I went and looked out through the parlour window. Roy was outside walking across the front porch. He had taken Grandpap's shotgun off the wall.

"He hid the money under that brush pile," Boann said. She was standing behind me looking after Roy. "Them fools is burning up their own money." She laughed.

The shotgun exploded. Before they grabbed him, Roy sprayed four men with buckshot. He kept hollering all the while they wrestled with him. By the time they finally understood what he was saying, the money was ashes.

When I looked back at Boann she was already moving past me. "Goodbye, Billy Watt," she said and walked out the front door, straight and tall as King Solomon's queen.

Boann moved over to where Georgie stood in the firelight with only one man holding him. The rest were fighting Roy. Georgie was naked to the waist, sweating and dirty, with a patch of tar on his chest and one on his face.

The man holding Georgie looked uneasy when Boann came up to him. Pretty soon he let go of Georgie. Boann and Georgie walked off together toward Gobbler's Knob.

I sat down on the porch and, while the men tarred and feathered Roy, I thought how the only difference between me and that lucky son-of-a-bitch Georgie was that he knew when to let go.

Luther

He closed the door and stood pressed against it, dripping from the rain, while he looked at her in the bed.

"Sunfish is over its banks," he said. "It's a bad lookout for the doctor's getting here soon if at all."

She nodded, staring away from him into the mirror over the mantle.

He took off his cap and slapped it against his thigh and the water flew. He remained against the door, cap in hand.

She gave a squirm and a wiggle under the covers.

"Ah godsake, Jack," she said. "Sit down. You put me crazy standing there mooning."

He took off his slicker and hung it and his cap on a peg in the entry. He kicked off his rubber boots and placed them underneath the coat. Then he came and sat in his chair beside the bed.

This child of theirs wanted to come into the world but something was keeping it back.

He looked at Lu lying in the bed where he himself had been born and his father and his grandfather. None of the births had required a doctor. But here was Lu needing one. She was different in everything.

"When the child is born," Lu said, still not looking at him, looking into the mirror that had been hung there by his great-grandmother, "I'll take it and leave."

"So you've said."

He couldn't argue with her. Let her say what she wanted to say. Still if she left, the child would stay.

He stood up, wrung out the rag in the basin and wiped her face for her. She was sweating a lot. His sisters' hair was long and straight and fair. It was very heavy. But Lu's was curly and dark and thin. She cut it herself so it framed her face. But now it was tumbled and wet and stuck to her forehead.

"The room's so close," she said. "I'm smothering for a good breath."

"The rain makes it."

But she said the same on sunny days. She was always smothering for a good breath in this house.

"I care for you, Jack, and I'd like to stay," she said, "but I must take the child away so it won't smother."

He listened to her voice more than to her words and heard it catch and knew she was having the pains again. He leant forward looking out the window, hoping to see the doctor coming through the rain. The daylight was beginning to fade away.

She closed her eyes and breathed fast, moaning a little.

It was all right with him if she left. But the baby stayed, since it was a Fergus.

After the dark came, he brought in a bit of wood and a handful of dry kindling and made a fire in the grate.

He didn't light a lamp since she seemed to be sleeping.

The firelight reached up to the plates set on edge in the cupboard and played amongst them like red fingers. He took comfort in looking at the plates. The blue ones with the hunting scene had belonged to his great-grandmother. He'd eaten off those plates since he had been a child. His father and his grandfather had eaten off them, too. Looking at the plates, he almost dozed.

"Why are you sitting in the dark, Jack?" she said all at once so that he started.

He lit the lamp by the bed. Still, nothing would do but he must light all three lamps in the room.

"It's always dark in here," she said. "There's never enough light."

His sisters said Lu was wasteful.

"She'll make you a poor man, Jack," Mary Agnes had said when she'd seen how Lu kept all the lamps lit of a night even in the daylight hours.

The child was coming early else Susan or Mary Agnes would be here to help. They were to come starting Monday, turn and turn about since they each had families of their own to do for. He looked forward to their coming because they would set the house right. Lu kept things all of a jumble. But she was young.

"This is a man-child, I think," Lu said, panting a little, "because he pounds me so. I'll call him Dermot. That means 'freeman.' I'll call him Dermot so no one can own him."

He turned his head away. She had been spouting outlandish names since first she knew the child was coming. She had a book of them she read of an evening. However, the boy, if so it was, would be called John Earle Fergus and would be the fifth to bear that name. It would be written down *John Earle Fergus V* in the family Bible. He had told her so.

He got up and fetched his pipe and tobacco from the mantle. In the mirror he looked into his own eyes for a moment as he picked up his smoking things. All the Fergus men held a close resemblance each to the other. They were all tall and heavy-shouldered with blue eyes and light hair. He wore a mustache as his father had before him.

They were all alike in character, too. All the country knew what to expect of a Fergus. They gave fair measure in a trade, paid their debts and stood by their neighbors. Their word was as good as a contract written in ink.

He sat down with a sigh. No Fergus had ever parted with his wife. Still, if she left, the blame for that would be at her door. It was well known she was scatter-brained.

He had misjudged in marrying her, right enough. His sisters themselves said so. Yet she was a pert little thing and it hurt him to see her suffer so.

He kept a watch through the window, puffing slowly on his pipe. She lay quiet, saying nothing.

"Doc's had time and twice over to be here since I called," Jack said. "He was starting right out."

She didn't speak but lay with her head turned away.

The first year of their marriage she talked a blue streak. He could make no head nor tail of it. Of late she had turned more and more silent.

He saw she was looking at the mirror again. He knew she disliked it.

"It's old as the hills and the glass is gone bad," she said. "A body looks pulled out of shape in it and the color of a corpse."

But he said it had always hung over the mantle and the house wouldn't be the same without it. A new one wouldn't do. You couldn't buy a mirror framed in gilt now, not with hand-painted flowers.

The pains took her suddenly so that she cried out. He started to his feet.

Surely she ought to be making more progress. Mayhap the child was too big. Or else she wasn't working at the business properly but helter-skelter as she did everything.

"Look here," he said, "you must use the pains to bring things along. You must push with them, you see."

"Say, Jack," she said, "just you climb in bed here and do it as it should be done and I'll slip out and have a puff at your pipe and rest a bit."

He felt his face go red so that his earlobes burned. She could always mortify him. Here she'd cut him down to an inch high, in labor though she was.

He frowned and began scraping at his pipe bowl with the blade of his pocket knife. When he looked up, the bed was shaking so he thought she was taken bad again, but then he saw she was laughing.

Laughing! Her cheeks were all rosy and her eyes squinted up, looking at him.

He sat staring at her, scratching his head in wonderment, while the old tenderness for her came up in him so strong and so unexpectedly it nearly choked his breath.

"Whatever's come over you to set you laughing?" he asked her.

"I was thinking when we met," she said, "you told me how to dance in the same way you tell me how to bear the child."

"You didn't dance properly," he said.

"I danced a new style," she said. "By the next night everybody in the county was dancing the new way."

"I never cared for it," he said.

It was true they'd met at a dance. It had been held in the Grange Hall where Jack's father had been Grand Master and his father before him and so on back. Jack danced with all of the most attractive and most respected single girls there and he danced with his sisters. As he led Mary Agnes around in the figures of the dance she said to him,

"There is a new girl come this evening and she is a wild little thing. I think she is a gypsy."

"Who is she visiting with?" he asked because he knew no one had bought land or moved into rental property in the county lately.

"She lives in a trailer that's parked down to Sugar Grove," Mary Agnes said, thumping her feet in strict time to the music. "Her people just wander around. Her dad picks fruit or makes crops or does oil-field work. They're that sort. Her mother's a foreigner. German, I think. She doesn't know how to sew or make jelly. All she does is read books."

When the next dance started, and Jack was sitting quiet in his chair because he was tired, didn't this new girl come up and stand in front of him, laughing, with her eyes squinted up.

"Come dance with me," she said.

He felt his face go red.

"Girls don't ask the boys to dance here," he said.

"But I'm asking you."

He heard the other young people tittering fit to kill all up and down the row of chairs. In order to get away from them he swept her onto the dance floor.

"What do they call you?" she asked him. She was saucy and she talked an awful lot.

"Jack Fergus."

"I'm Luther Hadden. Pleased to meet you."

"Luther?"

"That's my name."

"That's not a girl's name. Girls are called names like Sarah or Susan or Mary Agnes."

"Well, but I'm called Luther. My mama named me Luther after a monk."

He changed the subject. "You aren't putting your feet right," he said.

"Yes, I am."

"No. Look here. One, two, three, then slide, four. Why are you jumping around like that?"

He said this last in a tone of alarm. They were beginning to jostle other couples and people were looking at them.

"I put an extra wiggle in it. See? It's more fun this way."

Jack suddenly found himself standing flat-footed in the middle of the dance floor while his partner backed farther and farther away from him, shaking her legs and shoulders in a way that attracted a great deal of attention from the other dancers.

First one couple then another dropped their arms and stood watching, open-mouthed.

They formed themselves into a circle around Jack and the new girl. The orchestra leader who was watching, too, craning his neck over a potted palm, began to pick up the tempo. Before long everyone was clapping in double quick time.

The first chance, Jack ducked through the circle and went to get himself a cold drink. His hands were shaking and sweat was trickling down his forehead.

He thought he was rid of her but it wasn't so. When he stepped outside to cool himself, there she came following him.

She had got herself a volley ball out of the recreation box and as soon as she set foot outside, she threw it right at him as hard as ever she could.

He had to let go his drink to catch it. The paper cup went sailing over the grass spilling pop onto his pants and shoes.

"Now see what you did," he said more in wonder than in anger.

He felt foolish standing in the moonlight holding a volley ball.

But she ran down the path away from him and turned and stood holding up her hands. He threw the ball to her. Then nothing would do but he must run past her and catch the ball when she threw it to him. Each time she caught the ball she waved him on. They passed completely across the field playing catch in the moonlight.

All during the game, Jack's face was red with mortification and he kept a watch on the door but no one else came out.

Then she overthrew him and the ball bounced into the brush at the edge of the road.

"Now you lost it," Jack said.

They poked about all along the fence but never came across the ball.

"Where does the road go?" she said.

"Down to the bridge and on into Sylvester."

"I'll race you to the bridge."

"No," he said. "Around here, girls don't race against boys."

But she ran by him in such a way he felt challenged and had to follow her. She got a long head start because he was slow getting under way. She was very nearly to the bridge before he caught up with her. She ran like a doe with her white skirt sailing out behind her. However, he got to the bridge ahead of her.

"I won," he said.

"I let you," she said. "I stopped to pick milkweed."

Sure enough she had her hands full of milkweed pods.

"I'd have won whether or no," he said, his chest heaving.

She wasn't breathing hard at all. She broke open the milkweed pods and blew the seeds out over the creek.

After they had stood still a while the tree frogs started again around them.

"There's a graveyard," she said, "up on the hill."

"That's where the Ferguses bury," he said. "All my people who're dead are buried up there. Where're your people buried?"

"They're buried in plowed ground and growing up into beans and corn," she said, "in fields from here to California. Some are in ditches by the side of the road. Some were burned and the ashes blew away. Some are underneath the sea."

She shook herself all over like a puppy and climbed down from the bridge and ran along the bank and stood close to the water.

"What do you call this?"

"Sunfish Creek. It's a crazy piece of water, though it looks sensible now. It floods its banks every spring. It spreads out over the countryside and washes the soil away. And people's houses sometimes."

She had got milkweed seeds on his trousers and he leaned over to brush the cuffs. The next thing he knew he was in Sunfish Creek, wet all over, struggling to get to his feet in the middle of it.

He looked up and there she stood on the bank, laughing. He was speechless. His face was on fire. He waded over and caught hold of her skirt and pulled her in. She made a large splash.

When she rose up, dripping, out of the water, she took him

around the neck with both arms and stood laughing up into his face with her eyes squinting at him. Then she stretched on tip-toe and kissed him on the mouth and while she kissed him she was still laughing because he felt her shoulders shaking against his chest.

And now here she lay, laboring to bring out the child, and laughing at him in the same way! And here he sat beside the bed in the homeplace under the spring rains as puzzled by her as he ever was. Suddenly he realized she had spoken to him without his hearing the words.

"What?" he said.

"Say, Jack, you'd such a funny look on your mug. What were you thinking of?"

"I was remembering the time you pushed me into Sunfish Creek," he said. "Whyever did you do that, Lu?"

She bent a close look on him and then gave a snort that set his nerves jangling.

"I wanted to see if you'd melt," she said.

Half-past eleven o'clock the bag of waters broke and she began hard labor. He was kept busy sponging her face and giving her sips of tea. Between the pains she slept, holding to his hand like a child. She was beginning to turn weak and tired-out.

Once, while he dozed, the fire went out. As he poked up the ashes and set on a fresh log the thought came to him for the first time that she might die. She and the child both might very well die.

He went at once, took the phone off its hook, and rang up the doctor again but there was no sound on the line.

"The storm's knocked the phone out," he said.

For a time there was no talking in the room, only the drumming of the rain on the roof.

All at once Lu sat up and pushed the covers off.

"Jack," she said, "I'm going outside."

"What?" he cried. "There's nothing but mud and rain out there."

"But I'll go out."

"It's been raining for four days. It's raining still. It's pouring, Lu. Listen to it pour."

"I don't care. I want to go out. I want to give birth to this child out-of-doors."

He saw she was taken with fever. Her teeth knocked together

and her cheeks were flushed. He stroked her damp hair where it curled over her forehead.

"Only wait until the rain stops a bit," he said. "Then go out. Go after the rain eases up."

He soothed her back onto the pillow and when he was sure she slept, he hurried into his boots and slicker and went a ways up the land looking in vain for the lights of the doctor's car. Coming back, he could hear the creek rushing by and make out the pieces of debris it carried with it.

When he took off his coat and boots his hands were trembling, but she woke reasonable and in her right senses. She wanted tea and she made him turn up the lamps.

"I'll call this child Adrian," she said, "so he'll always have plenty of light."

It was getting on for midnight. He got up and walked around the room and around it again.

"Godsake but you're all of a fidget," she told him. "What ails you, Jack?"

He sat down, feeling foolish.

"It's the rain," he said. "The rain wears on me. You know I hate flood time."

"We were married in flood time."

That was true enough. Though he hadn't planned it that way. Truth to tell he'd never planned to marry her at all. He'd never asked her. She did the asking, though he'd never admitted that to a soul, not even to his sisters.

"Look here, Jack," she'd said to him on a certain spring day. "Dad's moving on. I've got either to go along or marry you and settle here. Which had I better do?"

"Which would you rather?" he said, blushing.

So she stayed.

Mary Agnes and Susan did what they could. They arranged the betrothal dinners and the bridal showers.

The week before the wedding he came into the house to find Lu standing on a stool in the frontroom wearing his grandmother's wedding gown. Mary Agnes and Susan, their mouths full of pins, rushed him out of the house. But there came Lu following after them.

"Bad luck! Bad luck!" Mary Agnes and Susan cried out, taking the pins out of their mouths.

"Bad luck indeed if I must marry in this suit of armor," Lu said and stomped her foot under the heavy satin skirt.

"Our own mother was married in it," Susan said. "She looked like a queen. I can show you a picture. And I was married in it and so was Mary Agnes."

"It's got real chantilly lace," Mary Agnes pointed out.

"This dress is like a clam eating me," Lu said.

"It's the bone stays make it pinch," Susan said.

"This dress has swallowed me all, up to my eyes."

"It's a mite big," Mary Agnes admitted. "We'll take some tucks."

But the matter ended with Lu crawling out of the dress in her petticoat like she was hatching from a cocoon and she never let them get it on her again.

She made Jack take her to the drygoods store in Sylvester where she bought eight yards of unbleached muslin. She cut a hole for her head and sewed the two sides together and that's what she was married in. She had hepaticas stuck in her hair. She picked them on the way to church.

Since her father was gone, Jack's friend, Napper Dudley, gave her away. Jack had a great many strapping male friends, the best-looking and most respected boys in the county. They all thought it a huge joke that Jack was marrying a little gypsy.

After the preacher had read over Lu and Jack out of the Bible and asked them questions and listened to their answers, he pronounced them married and the organ played.

Jack was sweating like a plow horse. Mary Agnes and Susan and Jack and Lu stood in a row and all the people passed by them shaking hands.

Jack turned to introduce his new wife to a neighbor, and there she stood kissing Napper Dudley on the mouth!

Jack took hold of their shoulders and shook the two of them apart.

"Men don't kiss the bride at our weddings," Jack told Lu. "No Fergus woman lets any man but her husband touch her mouth with his after she's said her marriage vows."

Lu laughed up into his face. "I mean to kiss every soul, man, woman, and child in this church," she said.

And when George Howison came next through the line she kissed him on the lips with a loud smack that could be heard clear up in the sanctuary.

Jack took off his wedding coat and hit George a blow that sent him staggering back into the Sunday School room.

George's brother who was coming along following George through the line lammed Jack behind the ear and the fight was on in dead earnest.

Everyone, Jack most of all, agreed afterwards it was a disgrace and a scandal. Two pews were split and Napper Johnson's nose bled all over a hymnal. Even a few of the women forgot themselves enough to pull hair and scratch.

People talked about the Hadden-Fergus wedding for years, usually in whispers.

The reception at the Grange Hall went along more smoothly. There was rum in the punch and the men made up their differences. They embraced each other's shoulders and sang.

Lu carried a great bouquet of jonquils cut from the yard at the homeplace. She was supposed to throw it amongst the single girls at the reception but instead she ran away with it.

No one knew what to make of that, least of all Jack. He followed after her out the door and across the field and down the road. She was running and he ran after her, getting hot and winded. When he caught up to her on the edge of Sunfish Creek, his head was spinning.

"Where on earth are you going to?" Jack said jerkily out of his heaving chest.

Sunfish had burst its banks and spread over the fields. She stood ankle-deep in the muddy water.

"I don't feel married," she said.

"Jesus God Christ Almighty!" Jack said. He was surprised because the Fergus men never swore.

"I want us to say our vows out here where the water and trees are," she said. "I want to say my vows to you, and you to me without any preacher coming in betwixt us and without any church roof shutting out the light."

Jack knew he was married to a crazy woman. He stood staring at her.

She moved farther into the muddy water so it splashed up to her knees. She held her jonquils in one hand and reached the other hand back to him.

"Say, Jack, come on," she said. "Come into the water."

"What for?"

"I want us to stand with the water washing us while we say our vows. It'll make us bound forever because you kissed me first in the water and because there's earth, air, fire, and water and water's my element."

"Well, earth's mine and I'm not stepping off it," he said. "Not in these shoes. I paid twenty dollars for them and I've only just put them on today for the first time."

She kept reaching her hand to him, but he wouldn't budge. He knew from the last time if she got hold of him she'd dunk him.

"Come out, Lu," he said. "You can't wade in Sunfish at flood time."

"That's when I like it," she said.

"This is our wedding day," he said. "Be serious on this day if you never are on any other."

She gave him a long look. "I am serious," she said.

And she never moved to come out of the water and he never moved to go into it. So they stood apart and when the sun waned they began to shiver.

Lu dropped her bouquet and the both watched it going down Sunfish, spinning around and around.

When the young people from the reception came out looking for them, Jack was standing kneedeep in the water in his ruined shoes, thinking how the two most important hours of his life, the hour he fell in love and the hour he married, were spent sloshing around in Sunfish Creek. He was so mortified he wouldn't say a word to anyone. He didn't say much for the rest of the evening.

The marriage had its ups and downs. Lu was no beauty. She hadn't much chin and her eyes were too large for her face. She was so lively and quick she kept Jack's head spinning. But she was always agreeable and never cross.

Of course she'd no notion of housework. Every jar of tomatoes she canned the first summer went up. Besides, she was forever up to some foolishness that fairly took Jack's breath away.

One day she came to him as he walked over the plowed ground.

He was moving along with bowed head looking to see was the corn come through yet, when here she came running pell-mell down the furrow. He thought it was some child until she got near.

"Say, Jack," she called out, "I've been down to the Mayberrys and I took them a load of canned stuff from the cellar and they were tickled. The little kids danced a jig and Mrs. Mayberry cried."

"Out of our cellar?"

"Yes. Don't look so sour. There's cans and cans down there, I swear, Jack. Even some your grandmother put up and your mother. And cans Mary Agnes and Susan did years back. There's no sense in it setting down there. A lot of it's good yet but no one'll ever taste it. We put up new every year."

"The Mayberrys are trash," Jack said. "I told you before to leave them be, Lu. You'll catch some ailment going around them. Besides, if they're too lazy to can their own food, why give them ours? I don't understand you."

"I gave them some clothes, too."

"What clothes?"

Coats and dresses that have been hanging in the back closet since I came here."

"You never did that, Lu! They were my mother's clothes."

"She can't wear them up in the graveyard."

"I don't know what Mary Agnes and Susan are going to say when they see Mayberry women parading around in Mother's clothes. The Mayberrys are outside the law, Lu. They keep a still back in the woods."

Lu giggled. "I know," she said. "They gave me a snort. Pure corn, done in a copper coil."

Her lack of brains troubled him. Their children might be imbeciles.

"Godsake, Jack, don't scowl so. Your mug'll get stuck like that. Sit down with me a minute."

"What, in the middle of the field?"

"The ground feels so good. What's in this ground?"

"Corn. But it's not up yet. It'd better hurry, too, if it's going to make a crop."

"I can bring it up."

He had seated himself beside her, stretching his long legs out awkwardly. He looked at her and found that she was laughing up into his face with her eyes squinted against the sunlight.

"How can you do that?" he asked her.

The next thing he knew he was flat on his back and she was leaning over him nuzzling his face like a puppy.

He tried to roll away from her but she hung onto him and tickled his ribs until he laughed himself weak. Then she kissed his mouth and kissed it again and then again so that it stirred him and he gathered her to him and kissed her until they were both breathless.

He felt the sun hot on his pole and the earth they lay on was warm and the smell of timothy and clover was strong in the air.

"If we were back at the homeplace," he said.

"What's wrong with here, Jack. It suits me well enough."

"What, out in the fields?"

"It's better than the bed, for me. I always think all the old Ferguses are in there with us."

"Leave me alone, Lu," he said because she was unbuttoning his clothes. "Someone'll come along."

"There's nobody comes back here," she said. "Nobody but you and me. The woods are all around except for the pasture and there's nobody in there but white-faced cattle. Besides it'll make the corn come up. You'll see."

If anyone had told him earlier in his life he'd do such a crazy thing, he'd have knocked them down. When he rolled off Lu and looked up, his heart gave a leap. Six cows had come up to the fence and stood there looking at them, deeply interested. Jack felt his face growing redder and redder under the gaze of six pairs of curious eyes.

But the corn crop came on the best in ten years. And this child got its start.

In the bed Lu lay quiet for a moment and Jack took another turn out-of-doors. No one coming on the road. Rain still falling.

He walked down near Sunfish to look at some pieces of flotsam newly washed up. His heart contracted as he poked at the stuff. He recognized it as part of the bridge between the homeplace and Sylvester. The doctor wasn't coming, then. No help was coming at all.

He heard Lu screaming before he got back to the house. It was a high thin wail above the wind and rain and it cut into his soul. She lay with her body stiff and arching across the bed. Her eyes were dark as the night outside. He wiped her face and spoke to her but she never looked at him or showed she knew he was there beside her. She looked, instead, up into the mirror as if she had only to stare in it hard enough to see herself clear and true instead of cloudy and distorted as it really gave her back.

The pains were coming close and hard now with no let up. He could see her body shake with one and then with another and another. Her voice was turning hoarse from crying out.

He thought the time was come at last that he must see what he could do. No Fergus man had ever brought his own child, still there was no help for it. He washed his hands and got a stack of clean towels from the closet.

Many a child had breathed its first in that bed and never a stillborn or even a weakling among them.

He buttoned himself into a clean shirt and shook out one of Lu's fresh-washed aprons and put it on. He moved the lamp nearer by and turned back the bedclothes.

He could tell at once the child was coming wrong and there was the devil to pay.

He worked through the hours trying to turn it. He sweated his shirt as wet as if he'd worn it out in the rain. Sweat dripped into his eyebrows and down his cheeks. He straightened now and then because his back felt broken from bending over.

Still, what good could he do? His fingers were so large and she so narrow. He watched her face and knew for the first time that his own life would stop if he must let her go.

"Brace up Lu," he told her, and his voice shaking. "When this is done, I'll hang you a new mirror over the mantle and I'll cut you a window in the east wall."

He saw she had her teeth set tight together and that she was fighting to turn the child. He could feel her muscles working and working. She tried and tried. But he could see she was growing weaker.

He went into the kitchen, lit the stove and boiled a pan of tools: tongs and spoons and knives.

When he came back with the tools he thought she had died. Her face was grey and she lay limp with her arms slung out like a rag doll. But when he bent close over her he saw her breast rise and fall and when he felt the child, wonder of wonders, he knew that she had managed to turn it the least bit. And that least bit was enough to let him bring the child out.

It was slow work. He shifted her sideways across the bed and went on his knees between her legs and worked, with the sweat running off him, while the time passed. He worked until he grew weak himself and his arms and back and his fingers ached again and his sight clouded over with weariness.

But when dawn broke through the rain he held the child in his hands and drained its mouth and heard its first lusty cry. Bruised and battered as it looked, it was a sturdy mite, sturdy like Jack himself, like all the Fergus men.

He cleaned the child and wrapped him in a towel and laid him by his mother. He lifted her head back onto the pillows and covered her. She was breathing light and quick and her closed eyes were sunken.

He carried the tools and the bloody towels back into the kitchen. His hands shook as he laid them down and of a sudden his head swam so that he had to stretch out on the floor and lie there a long time.

When he was able to go back into the front room, he was astounded to find that Lu had raised herself on one elbow and had put the child to nursing at her breast.

She turned her head and gave him a close look and then she laughed.

He felt his jaw drop and his face redden. He'd thought to find her dead and here she sat laughing at him!

She lay back on the bed and, weak as she was, laughed until she cried.

"Godsake, Jack," she said, "you make a silly-looking midwife."

When the time came to enter the birth in the Bible, he wrote the baby's name down, *John Luther.*

The Wellspring

When Buddy came home from the army, he was afraid of the dark. There was no rhyme nor reason to the feeling but as soon as the sun went down his palms commenced to sweat and his nerves went all to hell. He got his medical discharge as much for that as for his ulcers.

Flying cross-country from San Francisco he was calm enough. It was when a train derailment made him get into Trent several minutes after midnight that he began to have trouble. He stood in the station shaking in his shoes. Every soul on the train had thought himself a goner when the cars jumped the track. Buddy had helped pry an old woman out of the luggage rack. He got a glass of milk to wash down his pills. Outside, he wished he'd drunk coffee because the wind had ice in it.

Trent was shut up tight. Buddy walked along the main drag with his suitcase bumping his knee listening to the wind whistle through the empty streets. On the outskirts where his Gramma Wheat's house should have been there was a Texaco station. He knew the place had gone for back taxes after she died but he had expected the house to still be there. A high octane pump stood where his mama's jonquils had bloomed.

Out on the interstate it was like walking at the bottom of a well. The hills were tall around him, timbered and inky black. Far up overhead a few pale stars shone. There was no way out of the night except straight through it. Before he had taken a dozen steps, his stomach was clenched and in spite of the cold the sweat ran down his back.

He knew Fowler's Mountain by its shape. At the top, the roof of his great aunt's home, its peaks and turrets, reminded him of a church instead of a farmhouse. Going up the hill he climbed into a lighter world. The air was fresh and when he stopped and looked back all the valley was featureless and dark below like the ocean.

The fields he'd come to till were there, though he couldn't see them. "Buddy, why don't you come on home and mind the farm," his Aunt Lou Fowler had written him. But not she herself. Since her stroke she couldn't hold a pen. Not Garth who was only six. But someone else who wrote a clear round hand that made the words look like ripe fruit. He wondered who.

Aunt Lou Fowler was asleep and his brother Garth was asleep. There were no lights. Above the house, thrust up against the stars, he saw the windmill. There it was, just as he remembered it, crouched on top of Fowler's Mountain, black and spidery as a giant daddy long legs. He could already hear the crack of its blades turning in the cold wind.

Buddy wiped his sweating face on his sleeve. For years he'd thought he was a man but that sound shut up time like a telescope and he was a kid again scared as hell of Aunt Lou Fowler's spidery windmill. Buddy went on up the hill but instead of rousing them at the house he let himself into the barn, climbed the ladder into the loft, and flopped down on his back in the loose hay. Because, Christ, he didn't want to be in a house. He didn't want to be that close to people. Not yet. People and the dark, that's what made his fucking stomach hurt. He covered his face with his hands and felt his fingers shaking where they lay across his eyes. The air around him smelled of dried clover. The creak of the windmill was muffled in the barn. He heard sheep moving below him before he slept.

In the morning a little snow fell. Buddy looked out of the loft and saw a girl sitting on the fence feeding a lamb from a bottle. She was a big strapping girl in her teens. Her shirt sleeves were rolled up above the elbows and the hair on her arms shone golden. When he climbed down the ladder and looked for her she was gone.

He went up to the house. His aunt was sitting in a rocker at the kitchen window and beckoned him in. She pulled him down, hugging him, so that his hat fell off and his face was squeezed against her breast. Garth stood in the corner drinking water out of a dipper, watching over the rim.

Buddy hadn't seen his Aunt Lou Fowler since her stroke. Her bright blue eyes were as he remembered them, and her silver hair and her smile. But he was shocked to see how heavily old age had come on her. She hadn't the use of one arm nor of her legs.

Oatmeal was set out on the table and as he poured on the milk, he remembered the girl and looked through the window. There she was again carrying two buckets up the hill. A pale plait hung down her back but the short hairs around her face had pulled loose from the braid and made a mist that caught the morning sun. While he watched her, a large striped cat ran up the girl's back and sat perched on her shoulder, washing itself. Buddy rubbed his eyes. "Who is that outside?" he asked his aunt.

Garth came wiggling in between Buddy's knees and commenced playing with the buttons on his shirt. "Aunt Lou can't talk," he said. "Outside, that's Margaret."

"Does she always have a cat on her back?"

"Yes. That's Gibbet. Margaret's from the orphanage. She cooks supper and takes me walks in the woods and makes me willow whistles."

Buddy came to Fowler's Mountain at lambing season and he didn't have time to take a good breath until April. He and Margaret delivered so many lambs he lost count. Then they docked and wormed the flock. He got used to seeing Margaret with her shirt and arms spattered with blood and Gibbet sitting on her shoulder. Margaret was a wonderful help to him. She was strong as any man he ever met. She worked by him long weary hours and never complained. She had a gentle way with the sheep so that they trusted themselves to her.

Nights Buddy slept in the loft and days when he had the time and the sun was warm, he lay on the roof of the hog house, dozing. If Garth saw him it was all up.

"Play catch, Buddy," he would scream, hooking his elbows over the fence and rocking back and forth. "Will you? Will you, Buddy?"

"Jesus Christ," said Buddy swinging his legs over the edge of the hog house roof. "Stop bellering, can't you? You make my gut ache."

"How come you stay in the pig lot all the time?"

"Because these pigs never pesters me to play ball. All they do is lay here and sleep and twitch off the flies with their ears."

"How's it going to hurt you to throw him a few?" Margaret said from where she stood under the windmill washing clothes in a zinc tub.

"Hell," said Buddy. He stood up on the roof of the hog house and held out his hands. Garth threw him the ball, shagging it over the fence. "This is the poorest excuse for a ball I ever seen."

"It's the onliest one I got, though."

"This ball looks a million years old. The goddamned cover is coming off of it."

"Margaret can sew it."

Buddy followed the arc of the ball from his hand up into the air down into Garth's hands. His eyes focused on Margaret standing beyond Garth, beating the clothes on the washboard, wringing them tight, shaking them out. The sun shone on her wet arms. Beyond Margaret, in the kitchen window, his Aunt Lou Fowler sat looking out. "Don't she give you the creeps?" Buddy said, suddenly lowering his voice and nodding his head toward the window. "Never talking?"

"She don't need to talk, Buddy," Margaret said. "You kin talk, and look what it's got you: stomach aches and nervous fits."

The ball sailed back and forth over the fence. Buddy scowled. "Don't seeing her losing ground every day bother you?" he said.

But Margaret shook her head so her braid danced on her back. "It just means she ain't got no time to fool away, Buddy," she said. "That's why she grabs us all the time like she does. It's hard for her to reach out but every day she works at it and every time she touches us, then she smiles. And, oh Buddy, I dearly love to see her smile!"

"That's because you're all of you crazy up here on this mountain," Buddy said. He threw the ball so hard Garth dropped it and had to chase it. "You all got the same simple grin on your faces, you and him and her. It's like you all belong to the same goddamned secret smiling society. And I'm blowed if I can see what you got to grin about. Here's you and Garth orphans and Aunt Lou paralyzed and struck dumb and you all got no money to speak of and not much to eat. And there's that rickety windmill ready to fall on the house first storm comes along and squash you like bugs. Besides the water's gone bad in the well. And there you all are grinning like a pack of idiots!"

"Might as well laugh as cry," said Margaret.

"Well, I'll find you a pure wellspring and I'll dig you a new well," Buddy said, "and I'll tear the windmill down. I'll plant you a garden and milk your cow but don't ask me to join your smiling. I know better."

"You don't have to join in nothing at all as far as I can see," Margaret mused. "You're too busy swallering your little pink and yeller pills and listening to your insides churn to even know who's in the world with you."

"How I live is my business."

"That," said Margaret, "ain't living."

Buddy gritted his teeth. He threw the ball over Garth's head and banged it off the washtub giving it such a jolt the water sloshed onto Margaret. Margaret tossed the ball to Garth and when he caught it he laughed out loud. "This ain't my ball," he said. "It's a orange!"

"Eat it, then," said Margaret, "whilst I sew up the cover." She hung up the last of the clothes and, fetching a needle, thread, and a thimble from the house, sat down cross-legged like a tailor under the windmill.

Buddy stepped over the fence, scattering the half-grown shoats so that they ran off squealing in all directions. He climbed up and sat on the top rail, yawning.

"But this here is your orange," Garth said. "It's yours from lunch. There was only one apiece and I et mine."

"That's all right. Eat it up."

Garth sat beside Buddy on the fence, peeling the orange with his thumb. He was a thin, delicate little boy with big eyes like Enid, their mama. His hair was dark and curled at the temples like hers and his smile was Enid's except now his front teeth were gone. "I'm going to be a Big League's pitcher," Garth said.

"You can't learn to throw a curve with a lop-sided ball."

"I'll be a pitcher, though. Margaret says so. She says I'm special."

"What makes you so special, does she think?"

"My orange trees."

Buddy hadn't been paying attention. He opened his eyes wider and looked at Garth. "Which orange trees is that?"

"The ones in my ears."

Buddy took his cap off and scratched his head. "I don't see no orange trees," he said cautiously.

Garth giggled. "They're inside. You got to get close and look down in. Margaret seen one growing there after I et my first orange. And others has come since. She says they're a sign."

"Well that's the biggest bunch of bull shit I ever heard," Buddy declared. He almost fell off the fence turning around fast to yell at Margaret. "You're filling Garth full of crap," he called over to her where she sat with the shadows of the windmill's legs striping her face.

"I got sassafras growing in mine," she told him, "from drinking tea and chewing leaves."

"What's Buddy got in his?" Garth asked her when she came up to them with the mended ball.

Margaret climbed two rungs of the fence and peered into Buddy's ear. "Pigweed," she said. "Buddy's got pigweed growing in his ears from sitting in the pig lot."

Buddy jumped down off the fence and grabbed Margaret's plait. "You're the sassiest girl I ever met," he said.

"That's a compliment I paid you," she cried, pulling away. "Pigweed's amaranth and that's everblooming. It's a sign. Folks that's got it ain't ever going to die. It's in there, honest. You just never knowed it."

"You're just chock full of sassy remarks, aren't you?" said Buddy. And he wrestled Margaret to the ground and Garth, beside himself, jumped on top of them both. "Margaret is so dumb," Buddy panted to Garth, "she don't know where people leaves off and plants and animals starts in. She thinks she's part toad and part owl and part sassafras root."

With a stiff yank, Margaret pulled Buddy's cap down over his face and while he clawed at it she slipped her hair out of his fingers and away she went across the yard with Buddy, mad as blazes, hot after her. Around the house Margaret ran and down to the cowshed where she balanced around the edge of the watering trough and then back up to the pig lot with Garth shouting all the while and Gibbet shooting around and around the yard her tail fuzzed up big as a coon's.

Buddy judged he had her when she came up against the fence but she sidled along it and over to the windmill and commenced to climb the iron ladder up the side. Buddy went up a rung and grabbed for her ankle. Then up another rung and almost got a grip on her heel but she was too fast for him. On up she went and he after her, panting for breath.

She climbed to the top and crouched there just under the turning blades, laughing down at him. Halfway up Buddy looked away from Margaret, down onto the roof of his Aunt Lou Fowler's house, and beyond that down the hillsides into the valley. He saw the setting sun raised up into the sky again as if by magic. There it blazed, dazzling his eyes so that he turned dizzy and had to hang on tight and lay his forehead against the cold iron of the ladder to keep from falling.

In the dark that rolled over him, he felt Margaret's hands on his shoulders guiding him down, shaking him awake.

When Buddy came in from digging the new well of an evening, Margaret had supper on the table and after they had eaten Buddy took paper and pencil and drew a picture to show how he was sinking the shaft and how many inches the drill had gone down that day and he put a line where he thought the water lay and they each guessed how many more hours of drilling it would take to strike it. While they talked, the dark came out from the walls and up from the floor like water rising until the only light was the flicker from the cookstove door dancing red across the linoleum.

Then Margaret lit the coal oil lamp and set it in the middle of the kitchen table and Buddy looked at each of their faces picked out by it: Margaret's and Garth's and his Aunt Lou Fowler's. It seemed to him the light in his aunt's face came not from the lamp but from inside itself and he remembered how she had rocked him when he was little.

At bedtime when Garth walked around the table and kissed her goodnight, Aunt Lou reached out her good arm and hugged him. Then Garth kissed Margaret and then Buddy. His lips on Buddy's cheek felt like butterfly wings.

"I'm down twenty-one feet and about to hit water," Buddy said early one evening just after supper, "but a goddamned bolt got lost off the drilling head and tomorrow's Sunday. We'll have to pay an extra day's rent on the well driller."

"The stores in Trent are open Saturday night if you got the energy to tramp down the hill," Margaret said.

Buddy scowled. "I got more energy in my earlobes than you got in your whole body," he told her.

"Help me tie up the tomatoes and I'll go along with you," Margaret said. "So I can carry you home if you give out."

They went into the garden they had made behind the house and Margaret tore strips from an old sheet and he held up the vines while she tied them to the stakes. She was quick and deft and always ready to tie before he got the vine lifted. When the last vine was tied, Margaret took the remains of the sheet and before he caught her purpose, knotted it around his ankles and away she ran down the hill past the new well shaft.

By the time he kicked loose, she was a quarter of the way down. He tore off after her going all out. The wind whistled past his ears. The bushes and trees went by in a blur. The blood pounded through him setting his skin glowing. He began to whoop and holler. His voice soared out over the valley and echoed back. He caught up with Margaret at the bottom of the hill just before the last dip and passed her, still shouting. She grabbed hold of his shirttail and pulled him off stride and herself with him so that their legs flailed and they stumbled down the last slope, fell and rolled together, gasping, in the long grass. Their hands and arms were fragrant from the tomato vines. The sweat from their flushed faces ran together as he leant over her and when he kissed her, her mouth tasted of salt.

They scarcely recognized Trent. The village was transfigured. Strings of lightbulbs covered with paper lanterns hung over every street and every street was full of people. "Look at them blue and red and orange and yeller faces!" Margaret whispered. "I can't name a soul amongst them, they look so strange like they came up from Hell or down from Heaven, one!"

A great breathing sound of talking and laughing beat on their ears. Buddy could scarcely push through the crowd. He took hold of Margaret's hand to keep from losing her. He couldn't find the hardware store. He dragged Margaret up and down while he stared open-mouthed at all the buildings.

"That's it there, Buddy," Margaret said. "Right in front of you. It's purple instead of white is why you don't see it."

Inside all was ordinary. He bought a nut and bolt and stuffed them, wrapped in brown paper, into his pocket. When he and Margaret stepped out the back door, there was the street fair again. A great circle of people was turning around and around the parking lot. A fiddler played while all the people lifted their feet in time to the music. "That's what they used to call the Old County Dance," Margaret shouted. "My ma and pa danced it when I was little." Buddy wanted to go back into the hardware store but before he could turn around both he and Margaret were swept into the circle and must stamp their feet and sing like the rest.

So then it was around and around, panting and laughing. Streaks of light and threads of sound. And hands. First the people clapped and then they hit their heels against the ground and a one two three four, around they whirled and took hold of hands and so around and around. When the fiddle sang the fastest an allemande began: right hand left hand and on around the circle. First Buddy took Margaret's hand and she passed by him and he took another hand and another. At last, his head spinning, he went with closed eyes grasping over and over again a hand that was always the same, always different.

Even when Buddy broke loose from the dancers, he wasn't rid of the street fair because nothing would do Margaret but he must throw baseballs in the stalls and knock the milk bottles down for her. He threw and threw until his arm began to feel strong and warm and alive, and then he rattled down all the bottles and Margaret clapped her hands and cheered.

"Pick your prize!" the man said but Buddy had another ball to throw and he kept that instead, wedging it into his pocket where it pressed against his thigh as he walked.

When they got out of town away from the colored lights, Buddy knew they had delayed too long. Night was on them. He let go Margaret's hand and his face and his palms commenced to sweat. "You and your goddamned milk bottles," he said, with his teeth gritted. "Now we got to walk home in the dark."

"What you fretting for, Buddy," Margaret said. "Ain't nothing going to hurt a body with amaranth in his ears. Anyhow the moon'll be up in a half hour."

"Traveling this interstate on foot," Buddy said, "is like tramping through a fucking open grave."

But she was right. As they went on, the sky above the hills grew lighter and lighter until all at once the moon rose full and bright and turned all the trees silver and the road into a river of light. Beside him Margaret jumped and twisted, lifting her feet and flinging out her arms. Buddy thought she'd gone crazy until he saw she was watching her moon shadow behind her, making it cavort on the road. He saw his own shadow moving. Then Margaret's merged with his so there was only one shadow for the two of them. He was uneasy until they moved apart and he saw his own shadow clear and to itself again.

The next morning Buddy got up whistling before daylight. He walked down the hill to the watering trough by the cowshed for a morning wash but someone was there before him. Margaret stood by the edge of the trough, her clothes in a pile at her feet, sponging herself with the water where it bubbled clear and fresh from the pipe. The rising sun shone red on her wet skin and he saw the golden hairs on her arms standing up with the cold. Gibbet was crouched on the edge of the trough, her neck stretched out, drinking daintily.

Buddy came up to Margaret swiftly and she saw him too late to cover herself but instead looked back at him motionless with her head raised like a deer. For a while they stood quietly. Then he reached out and touched her belly, small and round like a new melon, and the hair beneath jeweled with drops of water.

She moved away from him gently. "Well you caught me out and that's my own fault," she said. "But looking is all you'll do, Buddy." Then she threw back her head and laughed. "I came out here so's not to wake up your Aunt Lou with that squeaky pump," she said. "I didn't plan on giving a show." For here came the sheep down the hill for their morning drink and the cow and her calf out of the shed, all watching Margaret as they came.

"You got a fine body, Margaret," Buddy said and his voice was gone hoarse.

"I was the runtiest kid at the orphanage," Margaret said, "but all of a sudden I grew bigger than any of them. Folks as knew her says I favor my ma now. She was a tall big-boned woman."

Buddy felt that the dawning sun behind him was suddenly putting out the heat of noontime. It beat on his pole, on his shoulders, and on the nape of his neck. It flowed down his back into his thighs like boiling water and there was nothing he could do about it.

He saw Margaret narrow her eyes, watching him. "Was you ever baptized, Buddy?" she asked him all at once. He nodded, scarcely understanding her, and took a step closer to her. "Well, that don't count because you wasn't never baptized like I'm going to baptize you," Margaret said and before he could back off she grabbed him by the hair and pushed his head down into the watering trough. "I baptize you," she said, "in the name of all these here sheep and cows and in the name of this ironweed and them pink and red hollyhocks and in the name of Trent and Kimball County. You was dead but now you live; you was lost but now you're saved. Hallelujah. Amen." At every other word or two she dunked him so that by the time she had finished he was groggy and spluttering and mad as hell. Before he got the water out of his eyes and ears and mouth she had grabbed up her clothes and was gone.

When Buddy got himself dried off he was over being mad. Instead he felt ready to tear into the drilling with all his might. As he got out the new bolt and fixed the drill head, he thought, "This is the day I'll bring in the well." He sat back on his heels and shook his fist at the windmill. "Down you come," he said. "We're done with you, you old bastard!"

Buddy drilled two hours before breakfast. When he stopped he was down twenty-seven feet. He remembered to get the baseball and take it up to the house for Garth. They had a good meal. Margaret had baked bread and she cut the warm loaf and gave each of them a slice and she gave Buddy the heel. When Buddy poured out the milk, foaming and fresh, into the glasses, the wind blew in the door and lifted his hair as if a hand had touched him.

Once Garth had the baseball, he couldn't sit still. He left the food on his plate to run outside and toss the ball into the air. He was back almost at once pulling on Buddy's shirttail. "Come play catch," he said.

And nothing would do him but Buddy must come until Margaret said, "Leave Buddy eat. He's hungry and tired from drilling. I'll play with you a spell."

As Buddy ate he listened to Garth and Margaret calling to one another in the yard. When he had finished, he stepped outside and fed Gibbet the scraps. A strong breeze was turning the windmill, making it grind with a great deal of noise. Buddy's pants flapped against his legs. He saw grey clouds piling up over Fowler's Mountain and felt a drop of rain.

The sudden hushing of voices puzzled him. Margaret and Garth and the ball were gone. The quiet pigs lay huddled together and the sheep stood like stones sniffing at the wind. Buddy started across the yard, his shirt fluttering. He had gone only a little way when he saw Margaret coming up the hill. As soon as she stood in front of him, she reached out and gripped both his hands. "Garth just fell down the well shaft," she said. "He fell down all the way to the bottom. One minute he was there on the hill and the next he was gone."

Buddy could feel Margaret's body trembling. Her great shuddering came to him through her hands. It traveled into his hands and up his wrists and arms until he shuddered with her shuddering through his whole body.

It was Margaret who went down to Trent and gathered up the people while Buddy knelt in the nagging wind and called Garth's name down the well shaft. As he called, he wrung his hands. Margaret came back riding in the fire engine beside the Fire Chief, Fred Kimes. The siren was going full blast. Doctor Joe Bryant was close behind and all of the volunteer fire department. After the people in cars were there, the people on foot began to come, men and women and children straggling up Fowler's Mountain until nearly the whole village of Trent was standing around the new well hole craning their necks and giving advice.

Buddy had sunk the well on a plateau fifty or sixty yards down from the house, where the land and rock formation looked promising. Margaret had witched it with a peeled willow crotch and, though he put no stock in witching, the spot she picked coincided with his. On this plateau, under the heavy clouds, with a little rain dropping now and again, Buddy watched the crowd converge and the volunteer firemen shake out their ropes and collect their picks and shovels.

When the firemen began to sink an emergency crater down beside the well, Buddy was forced back from the shaft. He crouched on his heels on the edge of the crater and a numbness spread from his stomach up into his chest and arms and down into his legs so that he felt immobile and helpless as his Aunt Lou Fowler. "Hope to God it don't rain," he heard the men say to one another.

As if it had heard, the sun came out, then clouded over again. Sun and cloud. Sun and cloud. But the wind never let up and the windmill never stopped creaking.

"More men're coming," Doctor Joe Bryant told him. There the old man stood with his shock of white hair and his big stomach, looking and sounding to Buddy exactly as he had the day he delivered Garth into the world.

Buddy made a noise in his throat as if he had forgotten how to talk, he had been squatting there so long in silence. Then he said, "I dug Garth's grave. There it is. I dug it myself."

The men came pushing in between Buddy and Doctor Joe, demanding, "How're we going to go about this, Doc?" Their shoes and clothes were caked with dirt and they sank their picks and shovels into the ground at their feet and scratched their heads and swore.

"How deep is that well shaft?" Chief Kimes boomed out as he joined them.

"Twenty-seven feet. Didn't Buddy say twenty-seven feet?"

"Yes."

"Well then we've got to dig."

"Dig. Yes."

"Let's get some sense into this operation," Chief Kimes shouted.

"Hell yes. Every time I sink a spade somebody cracks me in the gut with an elbow."

"Let the chief talk though. Quit bellyaching."

"Somebody's got to organize this business and be pretty damn quick about it, I say."

"First," said Chief Kimes, "you three men help Doc work that oxygen hose down the well shaft and we'll give the kid some air. Then we'll dig in shifts of five until we get this crater down within a few feet of the bottom of the well shaft. Then we'll sink a lateral tunnel to where the boy is."

"Let's get the bucket crane from down in Trent at the Olan Plant."

"No. We'd have a cave-in."

"It'd go a whole hell of a lot faster."

"Let them go get it," Chief Kimes said. "We can use it awhile. Not for long, but at the top here."

"All I hope is that boy don't panic and try to claw his way out," Doctor Joe said, sighing. "That soft dirt'd bury him in two seconds."

"Don't the damned wind keep on and keep on!" Buddy heard the men say. "It's sure to rain. Look at them clouds."

"Let's get down there," they said. "Oh God, let's get on down."

The bucket crane roared up Fowler's Mountain. After it had deepened the crater, the men jumped in and dug with shovels until they were spent and shaking and coated with mud. Then other men took their places. The clouds overhead gathered and rolled up the sky. The wind cut and whined.

Buddy could see that the men worked with a terrible concentration, shoulder to shoulder, silent now for the most part, saving their breath, striving together, glancing at the sky now and again or at the ten-inch well opening. Just before dark, Margaret and the other women brought sandwiches down to the men and thermoses of hot coffee. A dozen coal oil lanterns were lit and as many carbide lights and through the night the men kept digging.

Time after time as the night went on Buddy started out of his strange immobility like a man from a dream and jumping down into the pit, began to dig with a pick or a shovel or with his hands, clawing at the dirt with his fingernails until sweat soaked his shirt and dirt matted his hair and crunched between his teeth. He dug furiously until the men came and pulled him away, shaking him gently, saying, "Lay off, Buddy, for godsake, lay off. That ain't the way to go at it. You'll cave in the works, sure."

After several hours of work, Chief Kimes called a brief halt. "The dirt's shifting down there," he called out. He stood beside the shaft in his undershirt, covered with mud, his hair sweat-glued to his forehead.

"How's the tube, Doc?"

"It's still open," Doctor Joe said tiredly. "Oxygen's still going down."

"Let's put down the hook," Chief Kimes said.

"What if it starts a dirt slide?"

"We got the oxygen tube down all right. If the boy could hang onto this hook, we could pull him out. Or if we would catch it in his clothes."

Buddy watched the men lower the hook and pay out the rope.

It went down and down twenty some feet then caught and stopped. The men pulled up, lowered again, pulled up. The rope rubbed, worried like a line nibbled by a fish. It tightened. A cry went up from the men. Then the pressure on the rope was gone. They lowered it again and again with no result.

"We'd best pull it up," Chief Kimes murmured at last.

"He took hold of it that once, though," the men said. "Did you feel it?"

"Maybe," said Doctor Joe. "Maybe it caught on his clothes. Anyway, he could never hang on strong enough for us to pull him out and seems it won't catch again."

Buddy stood on the edge of the crater, his knees shaking under him. His hands were covered with blisters. It was past midnight. The wind had fallen at last but the sky was still overcast. "This is taking too long," he heard the men begin to say. "This should be done quicker. In half the time. It must be too late already."

"He can't still be alive, you know."

"It's seventeen hours he's been down there."

"There ain't been no sign or sound for a god-awful long time."

Chief Kimes drowned them out, bawling, "We're down far enough. We can start to bore the tunnel."

"Buddy watched a handful of picked firemen begin the delicate business of putting down the lateral tunnel. The digging went on growing slower and more careful. Now only three men were working, lying full length in the earth, making a human chain, until only the last man's boots showed.

The three firemen who had been digging came out of the tunnel and stood with their heads together talking to Chief Kimes. Silence settled over the people watching. It was as if they held their breaths. Buddy climbed down into the crater. "How long is it?"

"Fifteen foot."

"You've about reached him then."

"Yes," Kimes told Buddy, "but the goddamned dirt's just shifted again. Their shoulders are sticking against the sides but they're afraid to widen it for fear of a cave-in."

Buddy leaned over and peered into the tunnel. "That's wide enough for me," he said, measuring it with his eyes. "There ain't none of your men small as I am. I could get down."

Chief Kimes took off his cap and blotted his forehead with his arm the while staring at Buddy. All the men looked at him and no one said anything. Finally Doctor Joe cleared his throat. "One mis-move and you'll kill Garth and yourself in the bargain," he said.

Buddy's palms turned clammy and his breath came short and quick but he said, "I'll go down."

"You'll have to go slow all the way and take care when you break through," Chief Kimes said, "or it'll bury you both for certain." Then he added in a lowered voice. "It's a good bet you'll not come out alive, no matter what you do. Just so you understand."

They tied a rope to Buddy's ankles and gave him a cap with a light fastened to it and he lay flat on his belly in the dirt at the bottom of the crater and crawled into the tunnel. It was a tight fit. He wriggled his body forward twisting along as a snake moves, pulling himself ahead with his elbows. The numbness was gone out of him now. He had good command of his body except that he underwent spasms of shaking because he was afraid. One inch, two, a foot, three feet. The sweat dripped off his chin onto his hands. He went forward slowly, slowly, listening for the crack and sign of a cave-in. The moist walls hugged him so tightly he could move forward only by a great effort. When he was forced to widen the tunnel at certain spots he dug until his hands bled. Buddy thought he heard a sound of dirt slipping and he froze, listening, but it was only his own breath rasping in his throat. He went on crawling down bit by bit, slanting toward the bottom of the well hole along mud walls that shone like living hair and that bore marks of the fingers and tools of the men who had dug the passage and who were standing above now watching and waiting. The imprinted walls were the last sight he saw before a clod of dirt fell on his cap and knocked out his light.

Buddy lay for a time in the dark, squeezed by the walls of the tunnel, not moving. Slowly he felt his limbs begin to stiffen and shake, his tongue cleave to the roof of his mouth and all his skin turn icy and wet. He was afraid to go on through the dark and he couldn't go back. He lay with his face in the dirt and a sob broke in his throat.

Almost at once he thought he heard an answering sound. He lifted his head, straining forward. He thought it came again. Panting hoarsely now, dragging himself forward with his elbows, he inched toward Garth: Garth somewhere ahead in the darkness wedged at the bottom of the well shaft. A quarter of an inch, a half inch. His thoughts focused so intently on Garth that his muscles began to cramp and ache as Garth's were cramped and aching, his breath came hard as Garth's was coming hard. He strained toward Garth with all of his strength until he lost the sense of the tunnel around him and even the sense of the dark. There was only Garth up ahead and his will flowed toward Garth and he could feel Garth's will flowing toward him like water running until he caught and contained the boy in himself and the boy contained him and there was no longer any separation between them.

Buddy continued his great straining toward Garth in the well shaft until he felt a tugging at his ankles and knew they were beginning to pull him back. At that he cried out and lunged forward so that the fingers of his right hand reaching out before him struck into a wall of dirt and crumbled it. Beyond he touched warm flesh. Buddy grabbed hard with another great forward lunge and a slap of both hands. Instantly a sharp pull at his ankles jerked him back up the tunnel into the open air.

Buddy knelt, stunned, at the bottom of the crater. Below him the opening of the lateral tunnel was gone, knocked in by the feet of the men who had pulled him out. The dirt kept rattling heavily down where the opening had been. Both Buddy's hands were still closed in a grip on Garth. The boy's eyes were open. He looked at Buddy and began to cry. Trembling, Buddy raised himself, lifting the boy in his arms. Garth's body was rigid as if he were a boy of iron. His jaw was clenched, his eyes bloodshot and remote. But there was no dirt in his nose or in his mouth. And he was alive.

They came to him then, the other men, leaping down into the crater from all its sides. They came shouting, their faces smeared with mud, their hair matted with sweat, their eyes bleary patches of white. They laid hold of him with their blistered hands and brought him and Garth together up out of the crater. Buddy looked about him, dazed and vague. Behind the men, looking over their shoulders, were other men and women and children. The hillside was filled with them. He stood in the midst of them.

Climbing the hill carrying Garth, Buddy was hungry and shaken, covered with cuts and bruises, tired out, and feeling mean as hell.

Margaret came down to meet them, shading her eyes against the rising sun. When she took Garth, Buddy saw the boy whisper in her ear.

The three of them went on up to the house together, Margaret toting Garth astraddle of her right hip. "He says," said Margaret, "that you've got pigweed in your ears, Buddy, whether you know it or not. He seen it whilst you was carrying him up the hill."

The Imprisoned Woman

The tower had once been used for storing wheat. Small slick kernels lay along the cracks of the floor. She heard a mouse gnawing them in the night.

The room was twelve feet by twelve feet. It contained an iron bed, a thin mattress with striped ticking, a blanket, a table, a chair. On the table was a pitcher and basin. A small piece of mirror hung against the wall.

Once a day at evening, a tin bucket of food was sent up. At a whistle she pulled the line tied to the bucket. After she had taken out the food, she let it down again. Every other day they sent up a water jug and a few candles.

The tower had two large windows, one in the east wall and one in the west. When she was first shut up, she had beaten on the walls and tried to tear open the door and to climb out of the east window down the rope tied to the tin bucket. However the door was reinforced with an iron grating as were the windows. The opening through which the bucket passed was large enough only for the bucket.

She knew it was a serious matter to be imprisoned. As the government had grown gradually more and more authoritarian, it became known even in her small village that many people were being arrested for crimes against the state. The government kept files on everyone.

It was also known in the village that the country was divided into regions of surveillance, each designated by numeral, each with detention and execution points, secret and shifting. It was said no prisoner was kept alive for long.

And yet the imprisoned woman was still alive. And no charge had been made against her. On the day of her arrest, the government police had spoken only one sentence to her.

"Your name will be called."

She picked her brain to discover her crime. She was not a political person. She could only suppose that a deed of her long-dead activist parents, back when rival factions existed, had been set down erroneously to her.

As the weeks in the tower passed and her name remained unsounded, the imprisoned woman settled into a routine much the same as she had known in the village, begun by washing her face, punctuated by feeding herself three meals a day, and ended by placing herself in darkness by blowing out the candle.

She had long thick hair the color of ripe wheat and she occupied many hours with plaiting it and arranging it on her head.

As in the village, so also in the tower, she took small notice of her surroundings. However, gradually, a pounding and sawing that came constantly from the hill to the west drew her interest. She stood at the west window watching trees being cut out of the woods nearby and dragged up the hill with ropes. She saw them split and the branches trimmed off. Holes were dug. Two stout pieces of wood were sunk into the ground and a third nailed across the top. Then a platform was built underneath.

As the imprisoned woman watched the nails of the platform driven home, her breath came short and her palms grew clammy with sweat for she recognized the structure as a gallows.

The next evening a rope with a noose was placed on the gallows and all activity on the hill ceased. Every morning thereafter as the imprisoned woman bathed her face looking into the mirror, she saw the gallows over her left shoulder and every night as she stood at the west window unbinding her hair, she watched the sun set behind the noose.

As soon as she perceived the gallows finished, she began to listen in earnest for her name to be called. At first she listened only now and then. Soon, however, she passed into a state of sustained listening so that the business of listening went on even when she was thinking of and doing other things.

One day as she stood at the west window, the imprisoned woman noticed the wind, how it bent the wheat and how it blew through the tower smelling now of pine, now of the salt sea. Every day thereafter, she marked which scent the wind carried, in which direction it passed over the fields and whether it touched her gently or roughly.

On a certain afternoon the wind that darted into her face was full of tiny points. Soon she heard rain loud on the tower roof. Leaning on the windowsill, she watched the rain beating on the wheat fields and saw it move off toward the horizon straight and grey as marching soldiers.

Many times afterward as rain beaded her eyelashes or wind made the boards of the tower groan, she thought she heard her name called and was stricken with terror but she was always mistaken.

One day the imprisoned woman happened on a kernel of wheat wedged in a crack of the windowsill so soaked with rain that it had swelled and split and begun to sprout. Each day she observed the kernel, how the spear pushed up until it stood so tall it bowed in the wind and held raindrops in the green of its trough.

One afternoon a mouse ran out from the wall, darted up onto the windowsill, crouched and nibbled at the wheat spear.

The mouse's body was perhaps three and a half inches long. Its tail, another three inches, it held curled around in a half circle. Its fur was yellowish-grey streaked with black above. Underneath, its belly and its small feet were almost white. Where the sun shone through them, its ears were pink. Its whiskers glistened and twitched as its teeth gnawed.

She had never examined a mouse so closely. At supper she laid out a part of her food on the floor so that the mouse came to eat. She sat still, watching it.

Every day she studied the mouse. She learned the way its nose tested the air, the meaning of its different squeaks, and the manner in which its muscles moved under its skin as it ran or sat erect. Once she coaxed it into eating from her hand and as she looked at it, it peered back at her so that she saw her face reflected in its shiny black eyes.

All the while she listened steadily for the calling of her name since she thought if it did not come that minute, it would come the next and she was afraid she would not have enough time to learn all she wished to know about the mouse. She grew alert with watching and her face took on sharp edges.

One morning a bird alighted on the sill and pecked at the wheat spear. His feathers shone purple-brown and oyster colored. As he preened himself, his bright glance fell full on the woman and he stretched his neck toward her.

Watching the bird fly away, the imprisoned woman sighted other birds pushed by wind, wet by rain, dipping and soaring in the sky with their feet tucked up. She listened to the notes of their song, marked the curve and span of their wings and the patterns they made flying two together or four or twelve in a flock. When she looked beyond the birds, she saw the sky.

She began to wake early to examine the first pale yellow of the sunrise. It came softly as if a candle had been lighted under the eastern rim, then spread quickly wide and high. Sometimes the east turned the color of her own eyes as she saw them reflected back to her from the mirror.

Midday was shiny like the food bucket. Afternoons were blue-green. At twilight the western sky flushed behind the gallows tree and out of the east the moon rose blood red. Even the stars were coppery.

The imprisoned woman left her candle unlit to study the stars. She came to know many by their peculiar path, brightness, size, and coloring, and the patterns they made with one another. Their changing designs reminded her of the flying birds.

The moon printed the window grating sharply on the floor and the mouse played on the shadow and the claws of its feet clicked on the boards.

One day when she saw the mouse run across the floor, the imprisoned woman felt her own muscles move as if covered with furry skin and her own heart beat quickly at the smell of wheat.

When the wind blew in at the east window, her breath swelled in her body, lifting her breasts. When she saw the birds flying, her bones lifted in her flesh and she seemed to see far, a different view with each eye.

Watching the mouse, the wheat, the birds, and the sky, the imprisoned woman forgot to bind up her hair. She let it fall free about her face and down her back. The mirror collected dust.

She forgot to draw up the bucket and the whistle sounded again and again before she noticed. In the end, she forgot even to listen for the calling of her name.

She was surprised, then, one day toward evening when a key turned in the lock and two men in dark leather uniforms entered. One stood with his shoulders against the door while the other bound her hands behind her. Then they led her between them through the door, down the stairs, out of the tower.

The walk to the gallows seemed a short one. At once she was shoved up the steps of the platform where quick, efficient fingers dropped the noose about her neck.

A creak. A jolt. She lost her footing, pedaled air.

She felt her breath, and with her breath, herself, slowly squeezed from her body so that, thinning, expanding, she joined with the wind and swept like small rain across the hill and up toward a high rack of cloud. Looking back and down, she saw the tower standing brown as an empty husk and on the hill, the gallows, its rope pulled taut now by an unseen weight. About the gallows and the tower rolled the strange bright wheat, each blade stretching up, the tips beginning to lighten and shade into yellow.

She moved over the fields like a bird shadow, then, dropping, soaked dewlike into the soil so that she felt the wheat sprouting from her shoulders, the trees from her thighs while the early stars whispered her secret name.